The branch bent and swayed beneath Jane's weight; she lay there a moment, breathless, the rough bark digging into her hands. Twigs poked sharp fingers through the fabric of her dress. She peered through a concealing veil of leaves to catch a glimpse of the mysterious stranger. Movement caught her eye. Her breath quickened.

From what she could see, he was tall, but not overly so, with thick, wavy, golden brown hair. Biscuit-colored inexpressibles outlined his muscular legs. Athletic, well dressed, and probably wealthy, to boot. Who was he? If she could only see his face. . . .

She edged herself a little farther out onto the bough. The branch trembled. A colossal CRACK! split the air, followed closely by Jane's shriek. The tree limb, with Jane aboard, crashed into the rhododendrons on the other side of the wall.

Her shriek nearly sent the viscount out of his skin. He spun around to see what sort of catastrophe had landed.

No, not a catastrophe. A woman.

The Reluctant Rogue

Elizabeth Powell

A SIGNET BOOK

SIGNET
Published by New American Library, a division of
Penguin Putnam Inc., 375 Hudson Street,
New York, New York 10014, U.S.A.
Penguin Books Ltd, 80 Strand,
London WC2R 0RL, England
Penguin Books Australia Ltd, 250 Camberwell Road,
Camberwell, Victoria 3124, Australia
Penguin Books Canada Ltd, 10 Alcorn Avenue,
Toronto, Ontario, Canada M4V 3B2
Penguin Books (N.Z.) Ltd, Cnr Rosedale and Airborne Roads,
Albany, Auckland 1310, New Zealand

Penguin Books Ltd, Registered Offices:
Harmondsworth, Middlesex, England

First published by Signet, an imprint of New American Library,
a division of Penguin Putnam Inc.

First Printing, June 2003
10   9   8   7   6   5   4   3   2   1

To Jean,
my everlasting thanks
for the red-wine-and-French-bread therapy,
the sanity-saving pep talks,
and for being the best friend
I could ever have.

Chapter One

Over the past five years, Sebastian Carr, Viscount Langley, had come to the conclusion that there was no catastrophe so great that its impact could not be blunted with an excessive amount of brandy, and he was not about to let this morning's disaster negate that theory. His lack of available libations, however, might prove to be a problem.

The viscount tried to focus on the meager amount of amber liquid remaining in the decanter on the sideboard. Devil take that Corsican upstart. If not for this damned inconvenient war, Sebastian would have had enough of the exquisite French nectar to keep himself happily oblivious for days. As it stood now, yes, he might be drunk, but not nearly drunk enough. He'd have to start in on the blue ruin after this; if he'd had any foresight at all, he would never have polished off the last of the claret two nights ago. Ah, well. Foxed was foxed, no matter how one got there. He reached for the bottle.

Light glinted mockingly off the cut crystal, flinging

rainbows of pain into his tortured eyes. He winced, shielded his gaze, and squinted toward the window. Bloody hell! Had nature itself decided to conspire against him as well? What had begun as a fittingly gloomy day had somehow metamorphosed into a veritable ode to spring. A very bad ode, from the look of things, complete with brilliant sunshine, trilling birdsong, and flowers popping up everywhere. Egad, the only thing it lacked was a few frolicking nymphs. Come to think of it, nymphs would be a definite improvement. Sebastian grinned at the thought.

The gesture, however, quickly wilted beneath the sun's dazzling onslaught. His eyes began to water. This would never do. He thought about ringing for Grafton, his long-suffering valet (come to think of it, he had never known a valet who *wasn't* long-suffering, especially in his service), then remembered he'd sent the man out on a mission of vital importance. No matter. He could do this small task himself.

The viscount turned, and the room turned with him. Turned—and tilted at a rather alarming angle. He halted, swaying, palm pressed to his suddenly clammy forehead. Hmm. Perhaps he was more disguised than he thought; he seemed to move with all the grace of a pregnant rhinoceros. True, he did not have far to stumble in order to yank the draperies shut, but he did not trust the perfidious floor not to spin and deposit him on his backside. It certainly wouldn't do to greet his guests from that rather inelegant position. Not that they hadn't seen him that way many times before, of course, but according to the strict rules that governed Society, one could collapse in a sodden heap *after* they were gone, but not before. A pity, that, especially since he would be obliged to pay closer attention to those rules from now on. Sebastian swerved back to the sideboard, then with unsteady hands managed to drain the contents of the decanter into his glass.

He stared into the depths of his drink for a moment, brought the glass to his lips . . . and hesitated. No, the voice was still there. He had not managed to drown it out, though not for lack of trying.

If only you were more like your brother . . .

The words ricocheted through his muzzy mind with all the subtlety of cannon fire. Very *loud* cannon fire. The deliverer of those words had never possessed anything resembling diplomacy or tact, much less sensitivity, and this latest utterance was true to form. As far back as the viscount could recall, the only time his father had deigned to speak to him at all was to deliver some form of scathing criticism—with the exception of the last five years, when the man seemed to have forgotten about his heir's very existence. Not that Sebastian had minded, of course. For the first time in his life he had been free to live as he pleased, and he had made the most of it, if he dared say so himself. But that had all come to a crashing halt this morning when the earl had appeared, unannounced, on his doorstep.

If only you were more like your brother . . .

The words persisted, delivered in his father's clipped, disdainful tones. More like his brother . . . Sebastian made a rude noise. He would never be anything like Alexander—or should that be Saint Alexander? Given the reverent manner in which his father pronounced the name, divinity was a distinct possibility.

He knew full well he would never attain Alex's level of perfection. Not that he hadn't tried, mind you. Tried and failed time and time again, until he had grown weary of making the effort. Alex had been and always would be the handsomer, the more intelligent, the more accomplished, the more athletic, the more anything-you-could-possibly-name of the two. His father never missed an opportunity to remind Sebastian that he would stand forever in the shadow of his older brother, even when that brother was five years dead.

The corners of the viscount's mouth twitched. Actually, he had come to this conclusion on his own years ago; it had been painfully obvious to his then ten-year-old self. The revelation had been liberating, for only then did he discover how much easier it was for him to be a scoundrel than a paragon. Why make the attempt when he could never be something he wasn't? After all, one could not expect a leopard to change its spots, a fact that seemed to annoy his father to no end.

But Sebastian could not bring himself to say it. He had tried, wanting to fling the words at his father's expressionless face, to provoke some response—any response—but one glance from the earl's cold blue eyes and his tongue stuck fast to the roof of his mouth. He had stood in silence, face flaming, body tense, jaw clenched until he thought his teeth would shatter, while the earl pronounced sentence over him.

If only you were more like your brother . . .

Blast and damnation! Determined to silence the hateful voice, or at least muffle it into unintelligibility, the viscount tossed back a heady gulp, then coughed as the liquor blazed a fiery path down his throat.

A sudden burst of noise intruded on his maudlin musings, a combination of the violent creaking of unoiled hinges and a torrent of invective delivered in a patrician accent. Sebastian cocked an ear.

"I am not traveling one more step, you beastly little toad, until you tell me what the bloody hell is going on!"

The viscount chuckled. Nigel sounded rather out of sorts this morning.

"Calm yourself, my lord," Grafton cajoled in a soft, soothing tone. "As I told you, Lord Langley will explain everything. This way, please."

"Well, all I can say is that he had better have a deuced good explanation for rousing me out of bed at this ungodly hour," groused Nigel.

"My dear fellow," said a third man in amused tones, "to you, anything earlier than noon is an ungodly hour."

"And it is now half past eleven," Nigel huffed. "Barbaric, I tell you!"

Help had arrived. Good. If anyone could steer him in the right direction, they could. After all, what were friends for? With a lopsided grin, Sebastian propped himself against the sideboard and watched as two gentlemen made their way into his shabby, Lilliputian drawing room.

Lord Nigel Barrington shuffled in, appearing more like a figure from the commedia dell'arte than the younger brother of a duke. His straight, guinea-gold locks drooped over his forehead, and dark smudges shadowed the skin around his bloodshot blue eyes. His cravat, an intricate waterfall of pristine linen under normal circumstances, appeared as through he'd tied it in the dark. Wearing mittens. Sebastian tried to hide his widening smile; he knew the signs well. His friend was paying the price for the four—or was it five?—bottles of the questionable vintage he'd consumed at the gaming hell they had patronized last night. It was hoping too much, though, that an excess of spirits would improve the young man's taste in dress; this morning's combination of a mulberry jacket over a blue-and-lime-striped waistcoat made Sebastian want to draw the shades over Nigel as well.

Mr. Jason Havelock, on the other hand, appeared every inch the young Corinthian in his coat of midnight-blue superfine, buff inexpressibles, and tasseled Hessians polished to a mirror finish. Although he was not as tall or as handsome as Nigel (well, Nigel when he was in looks, that is), his tanned skin and dark, striking countenance garnered him more than his share of feminine admiration. And it appeared that he was the only sober one of the three. Well, at least someone had a clear head.

"Good day, Nigel, Jace," Sebastian said with forced good humor. He lifted his glass in salute.

"Well, aren't you cheerful?" grumbled Nigel. He collapsed none too gently into one of the worn high-backed chairs by the fireplace, which creaked in protest.

Sebastian waggled a finger at him. "Cup-shot, my good man, cup-shot," he corrected. "The only cheer in this room is the sort one pours from a bottle. I would offer you something, but I fear I've already drunk it all. Unless you're partial to blue ruin, of course."

Nigel turned vaguely green and shook his head.

Jace leaned one shoulder against the cracked marble mantelpiece, his brow creased in a thoughtful frown. "Your man said the matter was urgent, Sebastian. Am I correct in assuming it has something to do with why you're drunk as a lord? What happened?"

The viscount observed the curiosity on his friends' faces. He had known these two since they were at Eton, when the three social outcasts had little recourse but to band together against the bullying of the older lads. Black sheep, the lot of them, but their loyalty to each other had never wavered. Although they had had no secrets between them ever since their school days, it rankled that he had been put in this position.

Before he could say anything, however, Nigel blurted out, "Oh, Lud, you lost to Fairleigh. That's it, isn't it?" His lips curled in disgust. "The fellow's a Captain Sharp! I knew you were in the suds the moment you accepted his challenge."

"I think your words were: 'Devil take it, man, your wits have gone begging,'" Sebastian drawled. "But I did *not* lose to Fairleigh, and you would have known that had you stayed to watch, rather than sporting with that improbably red-haired Cyprian."

"You won? By Jove! How'd you manage it?" Nigel sat up in his chair, suddenly attentive.

Sebastian raised a laconic eyebrow. "You seem to forget that I cut my teeth at piquet. Fairleigh's method of marking the cards is so obvious even a child could make it out. He didn't seem to realize I was on to him until the very end, and the look on his face was worth more than all his vowels put together."

"Then why didn't you call him on it?" Nigel demanded.

"I could have, but I do not fancy grass for breakfast, thank you very much. Besides, the possibility that I might let this knowledge slip should be enough to prevent him from gulling anyone else—for a while, at least." Sebastian frowned and glanced down at his brandy. He was no longer slurring his words, and the pleasant, fuzzy sensation he'd cultivated seemed to be wearing off. Without another infusion of spirits, in a few hours he'd be sober as a parson on Sunday. Blast.

Jace cleared his throat. "Forgive me for being such a doubting Thomas, Sebastian, but you win and lose fortunes at the drop of a hat. Care to tell us what is this really about?"

"Very well, I shall come to the point." The viscount made a grandiose gesture with his glass. "My friends, I stand before you a condemned man. My esteemed father, the all-powerful Earl of Stanhope, has declared that I must marry before my twenty-fifth birthday or be cut off."

A moment of stunned silence greeted this pronouncement.

Jace recovered first. "Your birthday is but two months hence!"

"Exactly so. Two months to find a suitable bride, or I shall be left without a feather to fly with."

"But you bested Fairleigh last night," Nigel blustered. "And that was hardly for chicken stakes."

The viscount shook his head. "What I won is not nearly enough to make up for my string of reversals over the past six months. My father has me over a barrel and he knows it."

"You've suffered reversals before and come out on top," Nigel pointed out. "He's bluffing."

"Would that he were." Sebastian contemplated the last of his brandy, then finished it off with one convulsive swallow. Try as he might, he could not block out the echo of his father's derisive statements and the thread of steel that ran beneath them. "He is deadly serious, I assure you."

"Why now?" Jace wondered. "Forgive my impertinence, 'Bastian, but I find it odd that your father ignores you for the better part of five years, then suddenly barges into your life and makes this astonishing demand."

"No more so than I. I can only tell you what he said: that he has grown weary of paying my debts, and that it's high time I turned my attention to my responsibilities, namely, marrying and producing an heir."

"There are scores of unmarried ladies in London at this time of year," Havelock pointed out, "any one of whom would be happy to secure the title of viscountess."

Sebastian rubbed his forehead; his temples pulsed in rhythm with his heart. Was it his imagination, or had the close confines of his drawing room grown uncomfortably warm?

"Scores of unmarried ladies," Nigel muttered darkly, "*and* their mamas."

"How many of them come with a fortune?" Sebastian's voice grew rough. "I know what my father is doing—he has set these conditions in the hope that I will fail, allowing him to regain control over me. If I must marry, then it must be to an heiress; I'll be damned if I allow myself to be dependent on him for anything any more."

Nigel loosed an inelegant snort. "'Pon rep, if you'd gotten leg-shackled to that wealthy widow when you had the chance, you wouldn't be in this pickle."

Jace's booted toe shot out and clipped him across the ankle. "Stubble it, you oaf," he said with a growl, then shot a significant glance in Sebastian's direction.

"Ow!" Nigel shoved his chair beyond his friend's reach. "Well, it's true. She and her fortune would have been his for the asking, had Bainbridge not stolen a march on him."

Jace's scowl darkened; he and Nigel glared at each other until the viscount held up a hand.

"Cease and desist, you two—I have no wish to dredge up ancient history. And you need not concern yourself with my tender sensibilities, Jace. I have long since forgotten about Mrs. Mallory." Sebastian set down his glass, careful to school his features into a bland mask so his friends would believe the out-and-out lie. Kit—Mrs. Mallory—the Marchioness of Bainbridge, he should call her now—had been the first woman in a very long time whose company he actually enjoyed. Her wealth and unusual beauty had attracted him at first, but the few weeks he had spent in her company gave him an appreciation of her as a woman. But she had not loved him. Oh, she regarded him as a friend, something most properly brought up females would never consider, but nothing more than that. When he went so far as to propose marriage (a mad gesture if ever there was one!), she had hesitated. Perhaps she had even considered his offer for a second or two. But in the end she had graciously refused, even though the arrangement would have saved her reputation—not to mention his finances.

The news of her marriage to Lord Bainbridge last September had not surprised him; Kit had been head over heels in love with the dashing marquess. She still was. God's blood, anyone with eyes in his head could see that. He had spotted her in Town a few weeks ago, happy and smiling on her husband's arm, her belly beginning to swell with pregnancy. A strange, hollow sensation spread beneath his breastbone, but he shrugged it off. He could never have made Kit happy. Ultimately, a rogue like him cared for no one's happiness but his own.

"So, what is your plan?" Jace prodded.

Sebastian shoved his hands in his coat pockets, heedless of the way the fabric strained at the shoulders. "Gentlemen, I intend to take a logical approach to this dilemma. I need blunt, lots of it. And, somewhere in London, an heiress has her eyes set on a title. I propose a fair exchange."

"Egad, the thought of any of us leg-shackled to some simpering miss curls my liver," Nigel stated, shuddering.

Jace waited.

Sebastian paced a few steps from the sideboard, turned—and grabbed for the back of the threadbare sofa as the room seemed to wobble a bit. So much for sobriety! "Believe me, if I thought there was another way out of this dilemma, I would take it in a heartbeat."

Nigel leaned forward and stroked his chin. "What about the moneylenders?"

"I am already deep enough in debt without throwing myself headfirst down a well," replied Sebastian with no little sarcasm.

Nigel slumped. "Just a thought."

"Then what do you need from us?" Jace asked.

The viscount flashed a sardonic smile. "I have not had much contact with polite Society of late, so I need the names of heiresses in Town for the Season."

"I say," Nigel interrupted, "what if you were to marry a Cit's daughter? Plump in the pocket, but completely *outré*. Oho, wouldn't that send your pater into the boughs? Er . . . no offense, Jace."

"None taken. After all these years, you would think I'd be used to it," Havelock muttered.

Sebastian's hand tightened on the back of the sofa, his fingers digging into the thinning fabric. "No, not a Cit. I do not wish the earl to take exception to my choice of bride; that would be too obvious. No, she must be well bred in addition to well inlaid."

"Is the magnitude of the lady's fortune your sole consideration?" Jace wanted to know.

The viscount thought a moment. "She should be a comely chit—no diamonds of the first water, but no antidotes, if you please. I should hate to have to consummate the marriage in the dark."

A half-smile tipped Havelock's mobile mouth. "Anything else?"

"A sweet, biddable disposition would not be unwelcome."

Nigel guffawed. "Then for God's sake, stay away from Lady Blythe Daventry. She has fifty thousand pounds, but you couldn't pay me enough to put up with that shrew. Gives you her opinion on everything, then expects you to thank her for it. She cornered me at Lady Rowland's ball last week, and I barely escaped with my life."

"I would have paid good money to see that," Jace quipped, snickering.

Nigel ignored him. "There's also Lady Amelia Winthrop; she has fifteen thousand pounds, but she's a shy little dab of a thing. Can't say boo to a goose. And Miss Gray is fetching enough, but I doubt if she has two thoughts to rub together."

Jace rolled his eyes. "When did you become such an expert on heiresses?"

Nigel spread his hands. "Can I help it if ladies find me irresistible? After all, I am everything a woman could want: charming, handsome, gallant, well bred—"

"—vain, pompous, conceited, and ill dressed," Jace finished dryly.

"Ill dressed?!" Nigel echoed in outraged tones. "You wound me, sir. I'll have you know I am considered quite a Tulip of fashion."

"By whom? The desperately nearsighted?" Jace grinned at him.

Sebastian folded his arms over his chest and sighed. "Gentlemen, if you please . . ."

The two men exchanged one more good-natured glare and subsided.

"I have one last requirement," he continued. "I require the lady's fortune to be in excess of ten thousand pounds."

Nigel gaped. "Ten thousand? You *are* dipped."

"Yes, but not that badly. Once I have paid off my debts, the remainder will allow me to live quite well indeed."

Havelock remained skeptical. "A fair countenance, good breeding, a sweet nature, and ten thousand pounds—are you certain you can find this paragon in only sixty days?"

"I will find someone, Jace; if I have to sacrifice one or more of my requirements, then so be it. Beggars cannot be choosers and all that, but if such a paragon exists, I will make a go of it before I am forced to lower my sights. Within the next sixty days, I will find an heiress, wed her, bed her, and hopefully get her with child as quickly as possible. She will remain in the country to raise our offspring, while I reside in Town. I shall be flush in the pocket; she will be Viscountess Langley and eventually Countess of Stanhope. An even trade, wrapped up in a very neat package."

"An even trade, if a cold-blooded one," Jace mused.

"Cold-blooded? Highly sensible, I'd say," Nigel countered. "You may not have been born to the upper ten thousand, Jace, but you've seen enough of Society to know that among the *ton*, most marriages are nothing but contracts. In such cases it's far safer not to know one's spouse too well. Have you ever seen my brother, the Duke of Wexcombe, with his wife? Brrr. Now *there's* a chilly arrangement."

Havelock's dark gaze remained on the viscount. "I hope you know what you're doing."

"I cannot change what I am, Jace. The less time my wife spends in my company, the less chance we have to make each other miserable. So . . . will you help me?"

Jace's clouded expression did not waver. "All right, Sebastian; I'll help you. But I still think you're making a dreadful mistake."

"Oh, for God's sake, man, leave off your harping," Nigel scolded. "The situation is bad enough without you playing the role of the Greek chorus. You can count me in, Sebastian."

The viscount relaxed enough to smile. "Excellent. Now, before we begin in earnest, I suggest you get me out of this stuffy little hole in the wall and into a bottle of brandy."

"Jane."

What am I doing here? I don't begrudge Pen her Season, but I do wish Mama had not been quite so insistent that I come along to acquire some "Town bronze." Whatever will I do with it anyway, when I am going to do nothing but return to Leicestershire and marry Augustus? If she had been able to find a suitable chaperone, I suspect she would have left me back at Wellbourne. I should have preferred that. "Town bronze." Hmph. It sounds as though Mama wants to turn me into a statue. Well, she's too late. I'm already bored stiff!

"Jane?"

If only something interesting would happen! I vow we have done nothing but go to silly balls and parties where women simper and flutter their eyelashes at any remotely eligible man unfortunate enough to come

*within range of their claws. Last night I all but ex-
pected Miss Torrence to shout "tally ho!" and sprint
off in pursuit of poor Lord Rockhurst. Life in London
is a farce—if only it were half so entertaining. Drat it
all. I would much rather be back home; there is so
much work to be done. . . .*

"Jane Honoria Rutledge!"

Jane jumped.

Penelope's peal of laughter echoed through the confines of the small town house garden. "Honestly, dearest, you might at least try to *pretend* some interest in the
conversation. La, my own sister thinks me dull as dish-
water."

For the first time that afternoon, Jane was grateful for
the brisk spring breeze; at least it would cool her burning
ears. She ducked her head and made a great show of
smoothing the wrinkles from her poplin skirt. "That's not
true. Don't be ridiculous."

Penelope's laugh subsided to an indulgent chuckle.
"You have always been a terrible liar. You were thinking
about home, weren't you? Dearest, Mr. Finley can manage just fine without us for a few months."

"I was not thinking about Wellbourne."

"It is no use, dearest, you may as well confess—you
have not heard a single thing I've said, have you?"

"Of course I have. I . . ." Jane hesitated when she noticed her older sister's amused I-dare-you-to-deny-it
look. She bit her lip and smiled a sheepish smile. "Not a
word. I'm sorry, Pen. What were you saying?"

Penelope sighed. "I was asking you what you thought
of Lord Heathford."

Oh . . . the List. Jane snugged her wool shawl more
tightly around her narrow shoulders and tried to bring

some order to her jangled thoughts. Heathford, Heathford . . . which one was Lord Heathford? Lud, she could not possibly keep track of all her sister's admirers. "Well . . ." she hedged.

Seated next to her on the stone bench, Pen looked up from the small leather-bound book, pencil poised. She lifted one delicate eyebrow in a knowing arch. "You remember. The talkative gentleman with whom I danced the allemande last night at Lady Allenby's."

"Oh, *him*," replied Jane, and rolled her eyes. "The looby whose cravat was so tight it cut off the circulation to his brain. If only it had cut off circulation to his tongue as well."

Her older sister tried, unsuccessfully, to stifle her explosive giggle. "If you are trying to spare my feelings, dearest, it won't fadge."

Jane wrinkled her nose and grinned back. "Well, you wanted my opinion."

"Which is as brutally honest as ever," Pen acknowledged, still fighting her laughter. "But I had hoped for something a little more specific."

"All right, specific it is. Merits: Viscount Heathford is rather well favored, I will admit. He has very fine blue eyes. Drawbacks: he chatters like a magpie about the most trivial matters imaginable. While you were dancing with another partner, he proceeded to quiz me on your preferences for a gentleman's style of cravat. He then launched into an incredibly long-winded discourse on the advantages of tying one's neckcloth in a *trone d'amour* as opposed to *à oreilles de lièvre*, or some such nonsense. I had to plead a megrim in order to escape; it was either that or run shrieking from the ballroom. Anyone who marries that idiot will never get a word in edgewise."

Pen made a few scribbles in her book. "So noted."

"And what did *you* think of him?"

"I?"

Jane snorted. "You are not getting off so easily, Pen. I know you dislike to speak ill of anyone, but we agreed when we started this that we each must voice an opinion, even if that opinion is not entirely flattering. You have already heard mine—now it is your turn."

Her older sister shifted on the hard bench, her pretty features contorted in a grimace of distaste. "Of his merits—yes, I also found him handsome. His eyes are very fine indeed. But his drawbacks . . . he trampled my feet black-and-blue during the allemande and talked about nothing but himself and his tailor the entire evening. As much as I hate to say this, dearest, Lord Heathford has to be the greatest clunch I have ever met!"

"Oh, well," Jane murmured. "Another one out of the running."

The older girl finished writing and turned the page. "But enough about him. What about Lord Camden?"

Jane started. "Stay away from that one, Pen! The way he looks at you, the way he follows you with his eyes . . . he reminds me of a fox stalking a prized pullet. He makes me dreadfully uneasy. I cannot even give you anything for the Merit column."

A tremor shook Penelope, and she rubbed her palms briskly along her upper arms. "I agree. The last time I encountered him, he frightened me with the intensity of his regard. And I cannot overlook his terrible reputation as a rake and a spendthrift." She made several more notes. "I think we can take Lord Camden out of consideration."

Jane leaned over to look at her sister's scribblings. "Where does that leave us?"

"See for yourself," Pen replied, and handed her the book.

Ever since their arrival, Pen had kept a catalog of her beaux, complete with a column for the perceived merits and shortcomings of each, in order to make a more rational choice of a husband. And every afternoon the two of them sought out a quiet place in the house, well away from the curiosity of the servants (and the especially prying eyes and ears of McBride, their mother's dresser), to go over what they called the List. Today the lovely May weather had enticed them into the tiny garden behind their rented town house; dappled sunlight filtered through the leaves of the knobby elm under which they sat, and a lovely profusion of jonquils and crocuses bloomed in the sunny spot toward the center of the garden. The playful breeze twitched at the edges of their skirts and rustled through the elm's burgeoning cloak of green leaves. But all this vernal splendor could not distract Jane from the fact that so far their search was a dismal failure. She scowled and gave the List back to her sister. "This cannot be all the eligible bachelors you have met in the past six weeks."

"Well," Pen sighed, "these are all the *titled* ones I have met. Botheration. If only Mama were not so insistent that I marry a lord. I have made the acquaintance of several amiable, untitled gentlemen, but Mama would fly up into the boughs if I even considered a mere 'mister,' or even a younger son."

Jane noted the dejected droop of her sister's lips. Pen was right—and their mother's temper was legendary. She took Pen's hand and gave it a gentle squeeze. "We have been in London little more than a month, and we have over a month left. Give yourself time. I am certain you will find someone to your liking before then."

"You mean, find a *lord* to my liking. Why have I not hit upon the right gentleman? Something must be wrong with me, Jane. Or am I being too particular?" Penelope's anxious gaze searched her sister's face.

"Of course not," Jane replied with asperity. "It would be easier if you could select a potential husband like you would a horse—check the soundness of his legs, look at his teeth, judge his gait and his disposition—but in this case you're perfectly justified in being particular. After all, you will be joined to this man for the rest of your life, so you may as well hold out for someone whose presence you can at least tolerate."

"But what if I do not find anyone who wants me for who I am and not for my money?" Pen's question came out as a thready whisper.

"Stop talking nonsense. Goodness, you have half of the men in London at your feet already! Dozens of your beaux crowd into the drawing room almost every afternoon, and they send you flowers by the greenhouseful. You have to all but fend off the admiring throngs with your parasol when you venture out of doors. You are this Season's Incomparable, Pen. You will meet someone soon, I am sure of it."

And if she did not, Jane would eat her new bonnet, ostrich feathers and all. Penelope was an acknowledged beauty; her ebony curls, perfect oval face, and stunning green eyes attracted men by the score . . . as did her dowry of twenty-five thousand pounds. But she was also sweet, demure, and even tempered, if a little on the shy side. At twenty, she was perhaps a trifle old to be making her debut, but that could not be helped. Besides, her age seemed to matter only to the jealous misses whose suitors Pen bewitched. Although he possessed no title himself, their late father was the younger son of a viscount, and their family name went back to the age of Queen

Elizabeth. Pen *would* make a suitable match. It was simply a matter of finding a suitable gentleman.

Pen closed the ledger with a small sigh. "You are right, Jane. I must not let myself become blue-deviled. Still, I wish I might meet at least one lord who meets all our criteria. I am beginning to think no one like that exists." She paused, tilted her head to one side, and regarded Jane with a searching gaze. "But I still hold out hope for you."

Oh, no. Not this again. Jane averted her eyes. "Don't, Pen."

"Have you even thought about it? You have, haven't you? You're blushing."

Jane fought to extinguish the heat blooming in her cheeks. "Stop talking nonsense. I am betrothed to Augustus."

"That addlepate," Pen muttered. "And you are *not* yet betrothed, not formally. He has not come right out and asked you to marry him, has he?"

"He asked me if I would consider it."

"And what did you say?"

"That I would."

"Nothing more?"

Jane fidgeted. "Well . . ."

Pen's eyes rounded. "What did Mama say?"

"She looked me up and down and wondered why any man would ever want me."

"Oh, Jane." Her sister reached out a consoling hand. "Why did you not tell me?"

She shrugged. "Because I knew you would try to talk me out of it. I cannot afford to be a romantic, Pen."

"Perhaps, but that does not mean you must settle for the first man who offers for you! Especially a man who indulges in gossip and delights in ruining reputations.

There is still time to change your mind. Mama will not approve Mr. Wingate's suit until I am married off."

Jane concentrated on twirling a lock of her stubborn, straight-as-a-pin hair around one finger. Seeing her eldest daughter married to a count, a marquess—or even, in her wildest flights of fancy, a duke—was Lady Portia Rutledge's fondest wish. Her hopes for Jane, however, were another matter entirely. "With Augustus I shall be well settled, and with a minimum of effort."

"Oh, what fustian," Penelope persisted. "We are in *London*, dearest, and surrounded by some of the most illustrious bachelors in England! We have dreamed of this for years. You can do so much better than an overpadded, gossipmongering oaf like Augustus Wingate."

"It's not as though I have suitors throwing themselves headlong at my feet," Jane replied, more sharply than she had intended. She saw her sister flinch, then softened. "I'm sorry, Pen, but you must understand. Papa wanted me to wed a man who would maintain the stables as they are and help me to run them. I cannot marry someone who would do as he pleases with the land and destroy everything that Papa worked so hard to achieve. Wellbourne means the world to me, and I would do anything to keep it . . . even marry Augustus."

"Will you be happy with him, dearest? Truly?"

Jane shrugged. "Happy enough."

"Can you be certain of that?" Pen demanded. "Dearest, Mr. Wingate wants to marry you because his lands march with yours. He wants nothing more than to expand his holdings and line his own pockets."

"I know." The skin around Jane's eyes tightened, and her fingers curled convulsively around the smooth edge of the bench. Her sister had not meant the comment to be hurtful, but it stung just the same. No one glanced twice at a drab little thing like her when Penelope's beauty blazed so brightly. She realized from the moment he had proposed that her lands, not her looks, had attracted Augustus Wingate. "I am not looking to make a love match, Pen. My marriage to Augustus will give us both what we want. He will gain ownership of the property, but he has agreed not to interfere with my management of the stables. He barely knows a cart horse from a race horse."

A worried frown creased Penelope's brow. "Can you trust him to follow through, dearest?"

"We have an understanding."

"I wish you would reconsider; I hate to see you hold yourself so cheaply. There are other fish in the sea more amiable and broad-minded than Mr. Augustus Wingate."

Now that she thought about it, Augustus, with his slightly receding chin and round-eyed stare, did bear a rather pointed resemblance to a brown trout; it wasn't too difficult to imagine him with gills and fins. Not the sort of husband she had imagined for herself, but she must be practical. As plain as she was, she doubted she would receive any other offers.

Jane swallowed around the lump in her throat, then tried to smile. "We hardly need fret over my prospects, Pen, when we have our hands full with yours. At any rate, Mama would have my head if she thought I was trying to compete with you for a husband."

Penelope was not convinced. She frowned. "But—"

"Please, Pen," Jane entreated, "we have been over this before. Arguing serves no purpose; I have quite made up my mind."

"But at least consider someone else—"

Sudden movement caught the corner of Jane's eye; a prim, scowling visage disappeared behind a window on the ground floor. She held up a warning hand to stem the flow of Penelope's indignation.

"We had best go inside," she said in low tones. "McBride is becoming suspicious."

Pen's eyes widened with alarm. "Do you think she knows what we are doing?"

"I'm not sure, but I caught her eavesdropping outside your chamber door yesterday. She suspects we are up to something, and, knowing her, she will not rest until she discovers exactly what it is."

Pen paled. "If Mama finds out about the List, she will have fifty fits; she is still upset that I did not accept the Earl of Haydon."

Jane made a moue. "Even though he is seventy years old, gout-ridden, and smacks his lips whenever he sees you. For shame, Pen. He was such a catch, too." Observing her sister's distressed expression, she quickly added, "I was joking, you goose. All right, here is what we shall do: give me the List, then go back in the house. McBride is sure to follow you, so I will hold onto the List until it is safe to return it to you."

"Oh, dearest," murmured Penelope. She surreptitiously slipped the small journal to Jane. "You are the best of sisters."

"Make haste, before she notices we have made the switch," Jane murmured. "I will follow in a few moments." Turning her back to the house, she tucked the book snugly into her sleeve.

Penelope rose and took her leave; Jane watched her make her way back into the town house. She breathed a sigh of relief. The List was safe, for the moment. She rose, shook out her skirts, then wandered over to admire a patch of fragrant hyacinths that grew by the garden wall. She would stay outside a little longer so that Pen might send McBride on a merry chase. Rather like playing hunt the slipper, only with a slipper that would never—could never—be found.

Then a voice intruded on her solitude.

"Dammit, Alex, why did you leave me alone with him?"

Jane recoiled; her heart knifed sideways in her breast. Who was that? Heavens—the voice sounded like it came from right in front of her! She retreated several steps.

"He was never this bad when you were here," continued the voice, "but now . . . God's blood, I never thought he would go this far."

Jane gulped. The voice, hard, brittle, and definitely male, emanated from the other side of the garden wall. Who was this man, and who was he talking to? She edged closer to the brick partition.

"But I think I have found a way to get the better of him. He will never suspect. You'd be proud of me, I know you would."

Jane waited for another voice to reply, but the only thing she heard was the sound of the breeze rustling through the branches of the elm tree. She frowned. How very peculiar. When they had rented this house for the Season, Lady Arnholt had mentioned in passing that the place next door had stood empty for the last five years, something about a terrible tragedy. Obviously it was not empty now. Her heart slowed its frantic pace as curiosity overcame her alarm.

"I would never have had to resort to such drastic measures if you were here." The stranger sighed. "I miss you, Alex. I only wish I had had the courage to tell you sooner."

Who was this man? Did he have anything to do with the tragedy Lady Arnholt mentioned? Jane's better judgment told her to go back into the house, but something—perhaps mere curiosity, perhaps a reckless response to all the talk of marriage to pompous, trout-like Augustus Wingate—made her stay. Not only that, it made her want to catch a glimpse of the speaker on the other side of the wall. She had been responsible and dependable even before her father's untimely death; for once, she longed to do something—well—adventurous.

Lifting her skirts, she stepped up onto the stone bench beneath the elm tree. But even when she stood on tiptoe, she still was not tall enough to see through the decorative ironwork at the top of the wall. Drat.

Jane glanced back toward the house; she could see no one at the windows. McBride was busy trying to glean information from Pen. Their mother was not due back from her afternoon calls for another hour. Even so, remaining unseen would be tricky. She would have to move swiftly.

Several of the elm's branches stretched from their property into the garden next door. After tying her shawl around her waist so it would not get in the way, she took hold of the lowest limb, then used the knobby growths on the trunk like stepping stones and clambered her way up and onto the slender bough that arced over the wall. The branch bent and swayed beneath her weight; she lay there a moment, breathless, the rough bark digging into her hands. Twigs poked sharp fingers through the fabric of her dress. She ignored them and peered through the concealing veil of leaves to catch a glimpse of the mysterious stranger. Movement caught her eye. Her breath quickened.

As far as she could see, only one man occupied the overgrown tangle of vegetation that passed for a garden on this side of the wall. Had he been talking to himself, then? How odd. He stood several paces away from her hiding place, his back to her, his hands clasped behind him. From what she could see, he was tall, but not overly so, with thick, wavy, golden brown hair that brushed the top of his collar. His shoulders needed no padding, judging by the precise cut of his jacket. Biscuit-colored inexpressibles outlined his muscular legs so closely as to be almost indecent. His Hessians gleamed. Athletic, well dressed, and probably wealthy, to boot—all the hallmarks of a Corinthian. Who was he?

"Gads, I am getting maudlin in my old age. I had better get on with this before I lose my nerve . . . or my stomach," he muttered, and turned as if to leave.

If only she could see his face . . .

She edged herself a little farther out onto the bough. The branch trembled. A colossal CRACK! split the air, followed closely by Jane's shriek. And then the tree limb, with Jane aboard, crashed into the rhododendrons on the other side of the wall.

Chapter Two

The earsplitting CRACK! brought nerve to life. The subsequent shriek nearly sent him out of his skin. By the time the crash registered in his befuddled brain, Sebastian's body had already taken the initiative and spun him around to see what sort of catastrophe had landed in his lap this time.

No, not a catastrophe. A woman.

And she hadn't landed in his lap, but in Alex's rhododendrons. *His* rhododendrons, now.

Egad, had the Almighty heard his desperate prayers and taken to throwing women at him from above?

No, not a woman. He peered at her. A girl. Damnation. The figure struggling out from under the greenery appeared far too small to be a lady of marriageable age, and her serviceable gown more suited to the schoolroom than the drawing room. So much for divine intervention. The viscount studied first the injured elm, then the fallen branch. The chit had probably been playing in the garden next door, overheard his one-sided conversation (next time he would remember to temper the volume of his vehemence!), and climbed the tree to spy on him.

His jaw tightened. After the events of the last four-

and-twenty hours, an underdeveloped, overinquisitive little hoyden was the last thing he wanted to deal with. The ache behind his eyes increased to a full-fledged pounding, as though some demented Eastern monk had mistaken his head for a temple gong.

He straddled the branch, then held out a hand to her. "Are you all right?"

"Y-yes. I believe so." After a moment's hesitation, she slipped her scratched and reddened fingers into his.

Sebastian pulled her from the tangle of branches as though she weighed no more than thistledown. Gad, the top of her head barely reached his shoulder. He could not get a clear view of her face; her long hair, loose from its pins and hopelessly snarled, veiled her features. No matter. From her lack of stature alone, he'd wager she was no more than thirteen. Fourteen, at most. He leaned over her and scowled. "Good. Now you can tell me *what in the bloody blue blazes you think you are doing!*"

The chit backpedaled, slipping like a minnow from his grasp. "You need not shout at me."

The viscount's lips settled into a grim line. "Oh, no? First you have the temerity to spy on me, then you crash into my garden—which is private property, I might remind you. You trample my rhododendrons and cut up my peace, and I have no cause to shout? You could have gotten yourself killed and me along with you!"

"I'm sorry! I did not mean any harm," she protested, her hands bunched around fistfuls of her skirt.

"God forbid I should be in the vicinity when you do," he snapped. "Do you realize the trouble you could have caused me—caused us both? What if someone were to see us together? My servants have orders not to disturb me, but for all I know, your father, or perhaps a very large, very overprotective older brother, will come charging through the garden gate at any moment and demand my head on a platter for compromising you."

She lowered her head. "You have nothing to fear on that account, sir."

"Do I not? How fortunate." Sebastian didn't bother to temper the sarcasm in his voice. "You did not even stop to consider the potential consequences of your actions, did you? Zeus's beard, I've a good mind to do your governess a favor and paddle your backside here and now."

She gasped. "You would not dare."

He raised an eyebrow. "Are you so sure of that?"

She retreated another few steps, nearly tripped over a heretofore undamaged rhododendron, wobbled, but managed to stay upright with no further damage to either herself or the hapless shrubbery. What pins remained in her hair came undone; she brushed the loose mass away from her face with an impatient hand, then stared at him with wide, wary eyes. Sebastian stared back. Lud, what a strange little thing. Daubed in mud, with twigs and leaves in her disheveled locks, she seemed more fey than mortal. Her enormous eyes, gray-green like the sea before a storm, all but overwhelmed her heart-shaped face. Her nose was a trifle too long, her mouth a trifle too lush, her chin a trifle too sharp. She could not be considered beautiful, for her features were too irregular for beauty, but neither was she plain. Well, not exactly. Something about her drew the eye. The more he thought about it, the more she resembled one of the sprites from the illustrated edition of Shakespeare's *A Midsummer Night's Dream* he'd had as a boy. If he pushed aside that tangle of walnut brown hair, he fancied he just might find a set of small, delicately pointed ears.

His assessing gaze wandered downward. The insistent breeze snugged her gown against her body, and though she was small and fine-boned, Sebastian could see now that she was no child. Outlined in dirt-smudged gray poplin, her figure was that of a woman, slender and lithe, with a waist so narrow he could span it with both hands. Small, firm breasts rose and fell with her rapid breathing. Sebastian's pulse lurched into an erratic gallop.

"Well, imp," he drawled, "it seems I was mistaken. You are too old to have a governess after all."

A rosy blush stained her cheeks. Suddenly self conscious, she folded her arms across her body. "You are no gentleman."

Sebastian allowed a wicked smile to lift the corners of his mouth. "You should have thought of that possibility before you invaded my garden."

She raised her sharp little chin. "I did not—! You, sir, are nothing but a rogue and a scoundrel, and I take my leave of you." She lifted her skirt and began to walk toward the garden gate.

Sebastian stepped sideways to block her path. "And you, my dear, are a meddlesome minx who should be more wary of strange men."

She halted, her back ramrod straight, her slender body taut as a drawn bowstring. "Let me pass."

The viscount's smile broadened. "In a moment. We have something to discuss."

Distrust shadowed her eyes. "What would that be?"

"There is the matter of payment for the damage you caused," he replied lightly.

She glanced back to the twisted, truncated tree branch, guilt written on her elfin features. "What sort of payment?"

He heard the worry in her voice and almost regretted what he was going to do, but not quite. After all, someone had to teach this woefully naïve little country miss to

be more circumspect in her actions. "Don't worry, imp—
I am not after your pin money."

"Then what do you want?"

"A kiss."

She blinked. "A what?"

"A kiss," he repeated.

"Why?"

"Why not? At present I can think of no better form of
currency."

She stared at him with patent disbelief "You must be
joking."

"I never joke about so serious a subject."

"You want to kiss me," she said slowly, as if she had
not heard him correctly.

Sebastian fought back a stab of impatience. Egad,
from the look on her face he would swear the plaguey
creature thought him all about in the head! "I believe I
just said that."

"Then I shall ask you again—why?"

"And I shall give you the same answer: why not?" he
countered.

"That is hardly a valid reason, sir."

He planted his fists on his hips. "Well, then, why
should I *not* want to kiss you?"

"Because I am not pretty."

"Are you so certain of that?" He imbued the question
with all the persuasion at his command.

She flushed. "Come now, sir, let us speak plainly. You
do not wish to kiss me because you find me attractive.
No, no—please do not try to refute it or attempt to salve
my feelings with flattery. You would be lying, and we
both know it."

The viscount, who had opened his mouth to do just

that, closed it again without saying a word. Lord help him, this was the most unusual female he had ever met!

"I suspect you know a great many beautiful women who would gladly kiss you without protest," she continued, "so you must have another reason for wanting to kiss me. If I were to hazard a guess, you want either to frighten me or to punish me, or both."

Sebastian's brows rose toward his hairline. Most young chits, their heads filled with all sorts of romantic nonsense, would thrill to receive a kiss from a handsome lord, even though they had neither the wisdom nor the experience to recognize the possible motivations behind it. So how in the name of heaven had this one read him so easily? Perhaps she was a bit fey, after all.

"Did I guess correctly?" she prodded. She hesitated a moment, then grimaced and said, "Or have I just added insult to injury?"

"Well . . . yes, but I deserved it," he admitted. "And, yes, I was going to teach you a lesson, but now the point seems rather moot."

He thought he saw the barest hint of a smile slide over her lips, but he might have been mistaken. She met his gaze, transfixing him with a forthright stare. "Then I beg you, spare us both any further ignominy, and let me leave with what remains of my dignity intact."

His mind may have been flummoxed, but his instincts were still in perfect working order. Before he could stop himself, he said, "Very well. I will let you go for now, but you will still owe me that kiss."

"It is a debt you have no chance to collect, sir, for I sincerely hope we never see each other again."

Sebastian chuckled. "I would not count on that," he replied. "We are neighbors, after all."

Again, that half-smile shaded her mouth. "You need

not remind me. Good day to you, sir." With gazelle-like grace, she sidestepped him and hurried toward the garden gate.

"Wait!" Sebastian called after her. "Will you at least give me your name?"

She opened the gate and paused long enough to glance over one shoulder. "I think it best if I did not. I apologize for intruding upon your privacy and for damaging your rhododendrons. I have learned my lesson about eaves-dropping, sir; you made your point most eloquently. I shall not trouble you again."

Then she vanished into the alley.

Sebastian stared after her, totally and thoroughly baf-fled. That had not gone at all the way he intended; she had seemed affected by neither his looks nor his charm. Was he losing his touch with the ladies? Gad, what a low-ering thought!

Such a strange day this had been. He had awakened early—a little past nine o'clock—with gritty eyes, a wretchedly unhappy stomach, and a head that felt as though someone had wrapped it in wool and pounded upon it. Actually, considering the amount of brandy he had consumed last night, he felt better than he expected. Or he had until his father's man of business arrived, after which the morning took a decided turn for the worse.

With a superior sneer, the pompous little weasel in-formed him that he had been instructed to make sure Sebastian followed the Earl of Stanhope's orders to the letter, and to tell him the earl would brook no delay. The viscount had tried to reason with the chap but to no avail. Then he had tried ranting, swearing, and even threatening to be sick on the fellow's shoes, but the officious prig would not be put off.

Once Grafton managed to get him bathed and

shaved—no small feat, considering his rather miserable condition—Sebastian had made the journey to Hanover Square. Thankfully, as far as his woozy stomach was concerned, the drive had been brief. There he had taken possession of Langley House in order to fulfill the last of his father's stipulations. At which point he'd had the great satisfaction of ushering the little weasel out the front door and slamming it behind him.

Sebastian stared up at the rear façade of the town house. Cavernous and elegantly furnished, especially when compared to his shabby rooms in Half Moon Street, Langley House was just as he remembered it . . . except for the ghosts. His brother's presence lingered everywhere, from the portrait on the drawing room chimneypiece to the vague smell of cheroot smoke in the study. Everything had been preserved just as it had been before Alexander's death—a minimal staff had been kept on to maintain it with the greatest of care. Sebastian's lips tightened. This was his father's doing. He'd turned the place into a shrine to his dead son.

And now he expected Sebastian to live here.

The garden, at least, provided some solace. Alex had loved this place; he had called it his London oasis, a respite from the worst of the city's noise and the dizzying press of activity. This was the side of Alex that no one but Sebastian had been allowed to see, not even their father. Especially not their father. Though he had not much space with which to work, his brother had cultivated an array of flowers and shrubs that would provide color all season long, along with taller trees and bushes that would give shade on blistering summer days. A gravel-lined path snaked between the flower beds like a narrow, serpentine river. Like his brother, Sebastian felt at peace here. Or he had until *she* had tumbled into his life.

A most unusual day. The officious weasel, his dead brother's house . . . and now the irritating, intriguing, contradictory creature who lived next door. What else did Fate have in store for him?

Gravel crunching beneath his boots, the bemused viscount wandered back to the bed of bedraggled rhododendrons and knelt to survey the damage. Blooms, buds, and leaves lay scattered everywhere, but only two bushes appeared to be irreparably damaged. The gardener could easily clear away the branch, and replace—

A patch of periwinkle blue caught his eye, incongruous against the dark earth and shiny green rhododendrons. He drew it out from beneath a bush and realized it was a soft wool shawl. Hers, obviously. He brushed away the twigs and leaves, then noticed the soft scent that clung to it. Lilacs. The scent suited her. He chuckled, imagining the expression on the girl's face if he were to appear at her front door to return her property. But to do so would put them both in an awkward position, so he would have to find some other way to get it back to her. He fingered the material, then returned his gaze to the flower bed. Had she left anything else behind?

He looked more closely, remembering where he had found the shawl, then groped around in the damp mulch for several moments; his fingers closed around a small, rectangular object. He brought it out into the light and examined the cover. Some sort of journal by the look of it, although no identifying imprint marked the cover. The viscount rose and shook the last fragments of mulch from the book's surface. Perhaps whatever was inside would tell him the imp's name.

His conscience pricked him, but he shrugged it off. Once the girl realized that her diary was in his possession, she would be forced to see him again—and he could collect that kiss. Or at least he would tease her with the prospect. Sebastian grinned at the thought. What harm would a little flirtation do?

He opened the book. And frowned. What the devil . . . ?

On each page, written neatly in pencil, was a gentleman's name, along with a column labeled "Merits" and one labeled "Drawbacks." Some gentlemen had an equal number of entries in both columns, but for the most part their disadvantages outweighed their merits. He cringed at a particular turn of phrase; she had not been kind in her descriptions. His frown deepened as he flipped through the pages. Viscount Heathford, the Earl of Albermarle, Viscount Plimpton, the Marquess of Camden . . . all titled, to a man.

It seemed the girl was in the market for a husband, and she had set her sights quite high indeed. Sebastian closed the book and tapped it thoughtfully against his palm. Strange, then, that she had not played the coquette with him. She must not have known who he was. Yes, that had to be it; she had addressed him as "sir," not "my lord." Even so, his status should have been obvious . . . shouldn't it?

He glanced down at himself but found nothing objectionable about his appearance. He *looked* like a lord, one handsome enough to fulfill a girl's ambitious matrimonial dreams. So, even considering the — ah — unusual circumstances of their acquaintance, one would think she would have tried to take advantage of the situation; most of the marriage-minded females of his acquaintance certainly would have. Yet she had attempted none of the traditional methods of flirtation — no maidenly blushes, no fluttering of the lashes (although her lashes had been long and dark and eminently suited to fluttering), no demure lowering of the eyes. Curious.

Sebastian wandered back toward the house, still deep in thought. Who was this girl? And was there any chance she was an heiress? He snorted. Not likely; she had not been dressed in the first stare of fashion, nor, fortunately for him, had she been guarded by a dragon of a duenna. She seemed to be after a title, which might very well mean she was after a fortune, as well. He could not help her there. At any rate, she met none of his criteria for a advantageous match, so he should not even consider her.

He might not want to marry the imp, but she intrigued him enough to want to know more about her. He studied the neighboring town house. A few discreet inquiries would give him her name. She was in the market for a husband, which meant she would be out in Society; perhaps he might even see her at one of the many balls or parties scheduled this week. Seeing the expression of surprise and shock on her elfin features would be compensation enough for enduring the endless rounds of inquisitive stares and appraising glances from eligible ladies and their marriage-minded mamas.

As soon as the viscount passed through the back door, Grafton hurried across the empty kitchen to meet him.

"Is everything all right, my lord?" the valet asked, lines of worry etched in his narrow face. "I heard the noise, but you gave strictest orders that you not be disturbed . . ." He trailed off, his sharp dark eyes focused on the items the viscount held in his hands. "What on earth has happened?"

"Never mind. Grafton, my good man," replied Sebastian with a smile, "come with me. I have a job for you."

Jane hurried home, through the alley, back through her own familiar garden, and, after pausing long enough to ensure that none of the kitchen staff would see her, dashed headlong up the servants' staircase. She reached her room, closed the door quietly behind her, then leaned her forehead against the cool, painted wood. Her shallow breathing thundered in her ears. The scratches on her hands throbbed to the rhythm of her heart. An image of sardonic, deep blue eyes taunted her, no matter how tightly shut she squeezed her own.

She had never imagined that the branch would give way beneath her. Give way and throw her at the feet of a handsome, infuriating man. What on earth had possessed her to take such an absurd risk? The stranger had been right to scold her; she had not thought about the consequences of her actions. She butted her forehead gently against the door. Fool. Idiot. Addlepate. She could have gotten herself killed, injured . . . or worse. So much for her adventure.

Her whole body trembled as though her bones had turned to pudding. This would never do; she needed to regain her composure before her mother came home. Jane wobbled over to her dressing room table and sank into the chair set before it. She stared at her reflection in the looking glass and gasped. Heavens, she was a mess! Twigs and leaves stuck out at haphazard angles from her wild mass of hair, and a splotch of dirt mottled one cheek. She looked even more unattractive than usual . . . yet the stranger had still wanted to kiss her. Part of her had almost let him.

She shivered. Was it wrong to want to be kissed? Well, it was if the gentleman offering to do the kissing was someone other than one's betrothed. Besides, there was more to this stranger than an athletic form and endlessly deep blue eyes. Jane remembered the fine lines around his mouth and the puffy, slightly discolored skin beneath his eyes; she had seen such hallmarks on her father's face in the months before his death.

What vices and secrets lay concealed beneath the stranger's handsome exterior? And he was nothing if not handsome. Handsome—and arrogant and condescending and vexatious. Emphasis on *vexatious*. Yes, he had every right to be angry with her, but what sort of man kissed a woman to teach her a lesson? Whoever he was, she would do well to avoid him in the future; she did not doubt for a moment that, if they saw each other again, the rogue would attempt to claim that kiss, and how in the world would she explain *that* to her mother?

Jane picked up her comb and began to disentangle the bits of wayward greenery from her mousy locks. If she were careful, no one would have any inkling that anything untoward had happened to her. She would rearrange her hair, put on a clean frock, then go about the rest of her day as usual. She'd give the List back to Pen, and—

She stared down at the cuff of her sleeve, which was torn, dirtied . . . and empty.

The List was gone.

Her heart beating at a frantic pace, she searched her room, but nowhere did she see any sign of the small leather-bound journal. Where could it be? Had she dropped it during her flight back home? She dashed to the window by her bed, the one that overlooked the garden, threw open the sash, and leaned out. Was that it over by the rose bushes? No, that was merely a shadow. She scanned the garden pathways below until her eyes began to smart. Nothing.

Then the realization struck her. She knew exactly where the List was—it must have slipped out of her sleeve when she'd fallen into the garden next door. It was probably lying beneath that elm branch. Or . . . Her blood turned to ice. Or did *he* have it?

In a daze, Jane returned to her dressing table. How could she have been so careless? Oh, Lud, to think that she had lost something so important. If the List fell into the wrong hands, Pen's reputation would be in shreds by tomorrow morning. She shuddered and thrust the awful thought aside. She had to concentrate on finding the journal and getting it back.

But how? She could not very well march into the fellow's house and demand that he return Pen's List. Nor could she sneak in during the day and risk being spotted by one of his servants or, worse yet, McBride. Given the hawk-like way the dresser was keeping watch on both her and Pen, Jane would have no opportunity to slip out alone. If she were careful, she might have a chance to retrieve it tonight, after they returned from the Symingtons' ball. That is, if it was still in the garden . . .

She leaned her elbows on the table's surface, her hands clasped in fervent prayer. "Lord," she said softly, "I know I have not been myself of late, but please let me retrieve Pen's List, and I swear I will never, *ever* do anything forward or unconventional again. I shall marry Augustus and settle down to a quiet life at Wellbourne and never do anything the least bit adventurous!"

She had no way of knowing whether the Almighty heard her heartfelt plea, for at that moment a commotion from downstairs distracted her. Jane started; her mother was home. She swallowed hard. No one must see her like this, but especially not Lady Portia! Galvanized by a pressing sense of dread, she hurried to make herself presentable.

When she arrived downstairs fifteen minutes later, Jane tried to slip unnoticed into the drawing room where her parent sat chatting away with Penelope, but no sooner had she crossed the threshold than her mother's icy blue glare skewered her where she stood.

"And just where have you been? I vow you are the oddest creature, Jane, forever disappearing when I—" Lady Portia Rutledge paused, then inspected Jane from head to toe. "What on earth happened to you? Oh, do not tell me you were racketing about in the stables again. You're not a groom, Jane, but a young lady, and while we are in London I will thank you to at least make an attempt to act like one."

Jane bit back the angry retort that sprang to her lips; she had learned long ago not to provoke her mother. Instead, she gave a curt nod. "Yes, Mama."

"Were you in the stables?" her mother persisted.

"No, ma'am."

"Then where were you?"

Jane studiously avoided Penelope's curious gaze. "I . . . I was upstairs."

"I called for you a quarter of an hour ago. What were you doing that was so important?" Lady Portia demanded.

Jane bit her lip. As much as she hated to lie, no one could know the truth. "I was writing a letter."

"A letter? To whom?"

She blurted out the first name that came to mind. "To Augustus."

Her mother's eyebrows shot skyward. "That Wingate fellow? Do you not think that a trifle forward?"

Jane cringed. If only she had named someone else! Now she had to play through the charade and hope her mother believed her. If not, both she and Pen were in the suds. "We are all but betrothed, Mama."

"You are not engaged until I say you are," stated Lady

Portia, her lips pursed, "and until that time I must remind you to conduct yourself with a modicum of restraint. No more billets-doux — do I make myself clear?"

"Yes, ma'am."

"You are but eighteen, and Penelope, as your elder sister, must marry first. I will not tolerate any more willful disobedience, my girl. I am your mother, and I know what is best. Do not question my authority again."

"Yes, Mama," Jane repeated, her expression wooden.

"Come and sit next to me, dearest," Penelope entreated, patting the vacant stretch of striped sofa beside her.

Jane sat, then accepted the cup Pen offered her. The unspoken question remained in her sister's eyes, but she ignored it and sipped cautiously at the hot tea.

Lady Portia sighed. "You must learn to be more punctual, Jane. It is quite rude to keep people waiting, especially when it involves such a vital piece of news."

"Indeed, ma'am?" Jane inquired over the rim of her cup. Not that she needed to ask; gossip had become part of their daily ritual, and, judging by the impatient way her mother tapped one slippered toe on the carpet, she must be ready to burst with the need to reveal the latest tidbit.

"You girls should consider yourselves fortunate; you are among the first to hear this. I had it from Mrs. Ormsley, who had it from Lady Penworth, who in turn heard it directly from Sally Jersey herself, so it must be of the utmost importance."

Jane and Penelope exchanged a skeptical glance.

Lady Portia leaned forward and lowered her voice as if she feared being overheard. A smug smile curved her mouth. "A gentleman of great standing has moved into the house next door."

Jane's cup slipped from her fingers and rattled noisily against its saucer.

Her mother ignored the interruption. "From what I was told, Lord Langley may be only a viscount at the moment, but he is heir to the Earl of Stanhope, who is one of the richest men in England." Her tone oozed satisfaction. "Think of it, Penelope—we may well be living next door to your future husband!"

"But Mama," Pen protested, "we know hardly anything about the man."

"Oh, fiddlesticks," retorted Lady Portia. She stirred another lump of sugar into her tea with abrupt swirls of the spoon. "He's handsome, he's young, and he's the heir to a great fortune. What more do you need to know?"

"I would prefer to learn something of his character *before* I reach the altar," Pen said, a hint of reproach in her voice. "What is he like?"

"Well, from what I have heard, Lord Langley had quite a wild youth—he was quite fond of gambling and won and lost fortunes on the turn of a card. But Mrs. Ormsley said that the earl now expects his son to marry, settle down, and live the life of a respectable gentleman. That is quite enough for me."

"Then perhaps she should marry him," Jane whispered to Penelope. Pen giggled.

"Do not be pert, Jane," snapped Lady Portia.

Jane concentrated on her tea. "No, ma'am."

"Look at the hour!" Lady Portia gasped. "Come, girls, we have no time to waste. I am told that Lord Langley will be at the Symingtons' ball this evening. Penelope, you shall wear the white satin with the silver net, and I shall instruct McBride to dress your hair *à la grecque*. And you must wear no jewelry but your pearl necklace;

the viscount must notice you, not your adornments.
Everything about your appearance must be perfect."

Pen turned toward Jane and rolled her eyes.

Lady Portia set down her teacup. "Everything *must* be
perfect," she repeated for emphasis. "Jane, go upstairs
and help McBride press and lay out Penelope's things.
That should keep you out of trouble and out of the stables."

"Mama, there is no need—" Pen began.

Lady Portia cut her off "Nonsense. Jane has nothing
better to do, and I'm sure she wants to see you make a
successful match as much as I do."

"But—"

Jane laid a hand on Pen's arm. There was no use quar-
relling about this; their mother's word was law.

Lady Portia patted the very fashionable, very expen-
sive lace cap that graced her still jet-black hair. "As for
you, Penelope, you should go upstairs and rest. You cannot hope to catch the viscount with those dark circles beneath your eyes."

"I do not have dark circles beneath my eyes, and I do
not need to rest," Pen stated, her expression rebellious.
"Honestly, Mama, I am no longer five years old!"

Lady Portia's regard turned frosty; she pressed her thin
lips together. "When I was your age, Penelope, I was a
renowned beauty and could have had any man I wanted
as a husband. But I was forced to make a great sacrifice
for the sake of my impoverished family: I married a
wealthy man far beneath my station. Wealth, however,
signifies nothing without a title to go with it. I cannot tell
you the humiliations I endured—the cuts, the conde-
scension, the laughs and sniggers behind my back. I, the
only daughter of the Marquess of Ware, forced to marry
a—a farmer!"

Jane took a hasty swallow of tea, lest she give free rein to the angry, reckless words jammed in the back of her throat. Her father had not been a nobody; he may have been a younger son, but he was very well off and very well respected both in the neighborhood and in equestrian circles. But no matter how good a man he was, and no matter how good a husband, Lady Portia had never forgotten his lack of a title. Oddly enough, her father had doted on her mother—at least, he had until her indifference, combined with her flagrant disregard for his honor, had broken down his good nature and driven him to drink.

Lady Portia raised her head at a proud angle. "I have done everything in my power to make sure you have the advantages I never possessed, Penelope, and I refuse to see you waste your time on gentlemen who are not worthy of your beauty. You deserve to be the wife of a peer, and you will be if you follow my instructions. I am doing this all for you, can you not see that?"

Penelope ducked her head, but not before Jane glimpsed the tight set of her sister's jaw and the tears glimmering at the corners of her eyes.

She hastily set aside her cup and rose. "Come, Pen. I shall walk up with you."

As they ascended the stairs, Penelope linked her arm through Jane's. "Thank you, dearest. I do not know how much longer I could have listened to her go on like that. Please do not think me a goose, but if I dare say a word against her she will be in an awful pet for the rest of the week and make life miserable for both of us."

"I know," Jane said with a sigh. "She wants you to marry well, which is in itself a noble intention. I cannot be as complimentary about her methods."

"She is so resolute; she frightens me at times. Oh,

Jane, sometimes I feel . . . well . . . trapped. As if I have no control over my life any more."

"Don't be ridiculous, Pen," Jane remonstrated. "Of course you have control over your life! Mama can throw all sorts of titled ninnies at your head, but ultimately you will choose which one you want to marry—if you choose anyone at all."

Pen's fingers tightened on Jane's sleeve. "I have been thinking about that, dearest, and the most awful notion has occurred to me: what if she decides to pick a husband for me? I am not yet of age, so I would have no option but to marry the man she selects!"

Even though they had not been in London for very long, Pen had already refused two offers of marriage, much to their mother's displeasure. Given Lady Portia's determination, Jane would not put it past her mother to arrange a marriage for Penelope.

"Then we must find you a husband before the Season is out," she stated. "Surely there must be *one* titled bachelor in London who is neither ill favored nor ill mannered and has more weighty matters in his brain-box than the style of his cravat."

A thin smile appeared on Penelope's face. "I suppose we shall have to keep attending all these balls and parties so that I may add new names to the List." She leaned closer to Jane and added, "Is it safe?"

"McBride will never find it," Jane replied, with what she hoped was an air of confidence. Given the probable location of the List, that much was true, certainly. She gave Pen's arm a gentle squeeze. "I will return it to you tomorrow, I promise."

Pen smiled, then glanced downward and gasped. "What did you do to yourself, dearest? Your poor fingers are all scratched."

Jane resisted the impulse to thrust her hands behind her back. At least none of her bruises was visible! "I fear I was rather clumsy; I tripped on a paving stone and fell onto one of the rose bushes. I'm not sure who came off the worse for the encounter—me or the bush," she replied lightly. "That was why I was late; if I hadn't picked the leaves out of my hair, I would have received yet another lecture about my unladylike appearance."

Penelope hugged her. "Oh, my dearest Jane. Once we are married, neither of us will have to worry ever again about Mama's good opinion."

Jane smiled back, trying to keep the worry and heart-sickness from her face. Pen had entrusted her with the List, and she had let her sister down. She could not bear the thought of exposing Pen to censure and ridicule, much less Lady Portia's wrath. She had to get the List back before tomorrow afternoon. She *would* get it back, even if it meant the possibility of encountering the rogu-ish Viscount Langley once more.

That is, she would if nothing else went wrong.

Chapter Three

The Symingtons' ball, supposedly one of the great social events of the Season, reminded Viscount Langley of nothing so much as a giant aviary. Throughout the house, the crush of gaily feathered guests preened, posed, and paraded their fine plumage before one another. They cawed and chirped among themselves, identifying potential mates and assessing potential rivals. Here and there the chirping escalated into a minor squabble that ruffled a few feathers, but the well-established pecking order kept such displays to a minimum. On the whole, the flock seemed content to migrate from room to room, twittering in dissonant chorus.

When the butler announced his arrival, all eyes swiveled in his direction, and for a moment Sebastian was sorely tempted to turn right around and take himself off to a comfortable, smoke-filled gaming hell. But since he could not afford that option, he gritted his teeth and did his best to endure the squawking his presence engendered. Now he remembered why he so despised these Society gatherings.

"So, how does it feel to be back in fashionable Society?" Jace slanted Sebastian an appraising look as the three of them ambled toward the ballroom.

"Rather like I'm being eyed by a flock of vultures," replied the viscount with a growl.

Lord Nigel chuckled. "I thought you were here to play the part of the hunter, old boy, not the hunted."

Sebastian glared at him. "Tell *that* to all these dratted females. Egad, ever since we walked through that door I've been ogled by every single one, even the Dowager Marchioness of Edgebury, and she's eighty if she's a day."

"News travels quickly," Jace commented.

"Like the plague," Nigel added with an infuriating grin.

"It's disconcerting, I tell you." The viscount pasted a smile on his face and forced himself to nod to Lady Bartleby, who drifted past him in a cloud of patchouli perfume, fluttering both her fan and her eyelashes with equal fervor. The cloying scent nearly gagged him; he held his breath until the patchouli fumes dissipated. "Two days ago I was nothing but a wastrel; women would snatch their daughters away if I so much as looked at them, and my presence was barely tolerated in polite company. Now I'm considered a man of distinction, and those same ladies are throwing their daughters at my head."

Nigel snickered. "Makes it easier to catch them."

Sebastian ignored him.

"You're heir to a wealthy earldom," Jace pointed out, "and on an acknowledged quest for a wife. You should have expected this."

"If I had, you would never have gotten me through the front door." The viscount snagged a glass of champagne from the tray of a passing footman and took a large sip, relishing the effervescence of the tart vintage. "I suspect this sudden interest is partly my father's doing; no one else was privy to our discussion. I know the way he thinks. A few words in the right ear, and all of London knows about our agreement. And the more people who know, the more humiliated and ostracized I shall be if I cry off. He's a cunning bastard, I'll give him that."

"Careful, 'Bastian," Havelock advised. "I know that look on your face. Do not allow your anger against your father to prod you into doing something you will regret."

Sebastian's mouth curved in a mirthless smile. "Ever playing the part of my conscience, aren't you, Jace? Well, you need not concern yourself on my account. Remember, I have a plan of my own. Let's get to it, then. Nigel, see if you can spot a likely heiress for me."

Lord Nigel led them to the edge of the ballroom floor, then craned his neck and surveyed the crowd. "Ah . . . you see that Amazonian redhead over near the orchestra? The one who towers above her circle of admirers? That's Miss Hastings, from Yorkshire. Father's a baronet, I believe. She has ten thousand pounds, which is enough to make one overlook her rather horsey attributes."

"That is ungallant of you, Nigel," Jace objected. "You hardly know the lady."

At that moment, Miss Hastings threw back her head and gave a whinny of laughter that carried throughout the entire room.

Nigel hunched his shoulders and winced. "Then again, perhaps ten thousand pounds is not nearly enough. To think of having to listen to *that* for the rest of one's life . . ." He shuddered, then continued his scrutiny. "Now then . . . the girl in blue by the refreshment table is Miss Gray. I believe I mentioned her already. Fetching little thing, but she tends to chatter. And the reticent lady sequestered behind the statue of Cupid is Lady Amelia Winthrop. . . ."

Sebastian did not hear another word, for at that moment a vision of loveliness waltzed past. He stood transfixed, as though he had been struck by a bolt of lightning. A vision in silver and white, the lady possessed raven's wing hair, skin the color of fresh cream, and a slender, willowy figure. Her lovely face radiated perfection from the arch of her cheekbones to the delicate dark brows that flared over her green eyes. She tipped her head toward her partner and smiled, and Sebastian felt a sudden sweeping desire to taste those perfect pink lips.

"Who is that?" he asked, his voice hoarse.

Nigel followed the viscount's gaze; he brightened. "Oho! That, my dear fellow, is Miss Penelope Rutledge of Leicestershire, the reigning Toast of the Season. From what I understand, her father died about eighteen months ago, just as she was about to make her debut, but I daresay he left her well compensated for the loss. She inherited the sum of twenty-five thousand pounds."

"She is enchanting," Jace murmured, staring after the lady.

Nigel elbowed his friend in the ribs. "Close your mouth, Jace—you're gaping like a fish."

"So are you," Havelock retorted, flushed.

"Yes, but word has it the lady is after a title, and that leaves us both out of the running. What a pity. For a chit like her, I might be tempted to forswear bachelorhood."

Jace growled something under his breath.

"Does she seek a love match?" Sebastian asked warily.

Nigel shrugged. "To my knowledge, affection is not one of her requirements."

The viscount exhaled in a long, slow sigh. "Then she's perfect. Can you arrange an introduction for me?"

Lord Nigel replied with a cocksure grin, "Of course I can. One advantage of being an acknowledged gadabout is that I know almost everyone in London Society. A word of warning, though—be wary of Miss Rutledge's mother, Lady Portia. Very high on the instep, that one, with a tongue sharp enough to clip hedges. She tolerates me only because I am so very charming."

Jace snorted. "The fact that you're the brother of a duke doesn't hurt, either, of which you are well aware."

Nigel's grin widened.

Sebastian adjusted the folds of his cravat. "I'll be careful."

"Tally ho, then," said Nigel, and led the way through the crowd.

Miss Rutledge was not hard to locate; they had but to pinpoint the largest cluster of gentlemen. She stood in one corner of the ballroom, at the center of a throng of admirers.

Nigel shouldered through the crowd, heedless of the black looks thrown his way by the other eager hopefuls, and installed himself at the lady's side. "Ah, my dear Miss Rutledge! How delightful to see you again. And Lady Portia, you are as enchantingly lovely as ever."

Miss Rutledge dimpled. "Good evening, my lord. Mama, you remember Lord Nigel Barrington?"

The older woman arched a skeptical brow, then extended a hand to him as if she were the queen herself. "Of course."

Nigel bowed over her gloved fingers, then unbent and gestured to Sebastian. "I simply had to introduce you to my two greatest friends in all the world. Allow me to present Viscount Langley and Mr. Jason Havelock."

Was it Sebastian's imagination, or did Miss Rutledge's eyes narrow at the mention of his name? She smiled, but rather than offer her hand to either of them, the beauty dipped a graceful curtsy.

"A pleasure to meet you both," she murmured.

The orchestra struck the opening strains of an allemande; as if on cue, the viscount stepped forward and made an elegant leg. "May I have the pleasure of this dance, Miss Rutledge?"

"Yes, go on, dear," Lady Portia urged with an almost predatory smile.

"I—I cannot, Mama," the beauty protested. "I have promised this set to Lord Elmore."

"Penelope." Her mother said the name in a warning tone that raised the hairs on the back of Sebastian's neck. The older woman targeted her gorgon gaze on poor Lord Elmore; the baron turned pale and gulped.

The beauty unfurled her ivory fan and fanned herself with growing agitation. "I fear every dance has been claimed, my lord."

"Then I must be content to remain here and bask in the glow of your beauty, Miss Rutledge," the viscount conceded, reining in his disappointment. Obviously Lady Portia had heard the latest gossip and was in alt that he paid his attentions to her daughter. Miss Rutledge, however, did not appear to share her mother's single-minded enthusiasm. Had she heard the other not-so-flattering tales the London tabbies still told about him?

Then the girl straightened. "But there is one favor I might ask of you, my lord."

"Anything," Sebastian answered quickly.

"I believe my sister is without a partner for this set. Would you be so kind as to accompany her?"

Miss Rutledge had a sister? Younger or older? Whatever her age, if the beauty had to secure partners for her, then she was probably nothing less than an antidote. Sebastian suppressed a surge of irritation; if dancing with Miss Rutledge's sister would get him into the lady's good graces, then so be it. "Of course," he replied, his smile fixed in place.

"Do not do anything you will regret, Penelope," muttered Lady Portia.

"I cannot dance with two gentlemen at once, Mama." The beauty's words were brave enough, though her voice wavered. She fluttered her fan so violently that Sebastian half expected the delicate creation to break in two.

"Very well," Lady Portia huffed. "But we shall discuss this later."

Miss Rutledge sighed with obvious relief. "Jane? Where are you?" She glanced behind her. "Oh, there you are. What are you doing in the corner, dearest? Come, I have found you a partner for the allemande. My lord, I would like to present my younger sister, Miss Jane Rutledge. Jane, this is Viscount Langley."

She propelled a small figure forward, and Sebastian found himself staring down into familiar, changeable gray-green eyes. Recognition lit those eyes, and the younger woman gasped.

Sebastian made little effort to temper his smile of satisfaction. Well, *this* was unexpected! Never would he have imagined that the imp from his garden would turn out to be the sister of the most desirable heiress in London. A fortunate turn of events, indeed.

"I cannot tell you how delighted I am to make your acquaintance, Miss Jane," he drawled.

Clearly she had not anticipated this meeting, either; the expression on her elfin features told him that she would rather go to the guillotine than dance with him. His smile turned mischievous as he took her hand and bowed over it. "Cat got your tongue, imp?" he murmured.

"How do you do, my lord?" The arctic tone of her voice matched the chill in her gray eyes.

Sebastian chuckled. From the sound of things, she would like to send *him* to the guillotine.

Then he realized that her discomfort did not stem from his presence alone. She stood, her body tense, her lowered gaze sliding from side to side, taking in the amused glances of the assembled gentlemen. Her cheeks bloomed a fetching shade of pink. For a moment the viscount almost felt sorry for her; she looked for all the world as though she wanted the floor to open up and swallow her whole.

He glanced between the sisters. Petite and slender, they bore a strong resemblance to one another, especially in their height and complexions, but Sebastian had to admit that from all outward appearances, Miss Jane seemed but a drab and faded version of her older sister. Even dressed in a pretty gown of soft rose pink, she could in no way compete with Miss Rutledge's vivid loveliness. Most of her sister's admirers seemed to either ignore her presence or, worse, tolerate it in a patronizing sort of way. Small wonder she had sought refuge in the corner.

"Do not dawdle, Jane," Lady Portia snapped. "You must not monopolize Lord Langley's attention."

Sebastian caught Nigel's eye; a knowing look passed between them.

Lord Nigel turned to Lady Portia. "I must say, ma'am, the color of your gown is most fetching. Sardinian blue, is it not? Very few ladies wear it well, but on you it is captivating; it accentuates your flawless complexion. I vow that when I first met you, I mistook you for Miss Rutledge's sister."

The imp—strange to think she possessed so prosaic a name as Jane—stared in disbelief at her mother, who had begun to preen at Nigel's fulsome praise.

Sebastian offered her his arm. "Let us make our escape while we have the chance."

She placed her hand atop his sleeve, and he led her away from her sister's circle of admirers and into the assembly of figures on the dance floor. As they took their place in the set, the neighboring couples eyed them with barely disguised curiosity.

"Well, *this* is rather awkward," Jane muttered.

"But not, I hope, wholly unwelcome?" countered Lord Langley.

"That would depend upon one's point of view, my lord," she answered. "May I speak plainly?"

"Of course."

She squared her shoulders. "My sister, though she means well, takes it upon herself to recruit gentlemen to dance with me. For her, your presence is a welcome circumstance. But as for me, although I like dancing very much, I find myself torn between social convention and my own conscience, which remembers your conduct of this afternoon all too well."

"Ah yes . . . that," said the viscount with a slight grimace. "I owe you an apology, Miss Jane. I was not at my best this afternoon, and I fear I aimed the brunt of my ill temper at you. I behaved most abominably."

Jane nearly faltered in the middle of the dance steps. This arrogant scoundrel, who had yelled at her (deservedly so, she had to admit), mocked her, then demanded a kiss of her—was apologizing? "I . . . I am astonished, my lord," she managed to reply.

His grimace melted into a rueful grin. "What, astonished that I would beg your forgiveness? You must think me an unrepentant rogue, indeed."

Despite herself, Jane found herself smiling back. "I do not know you well enough to say whether you are unrepentant or not, my lord."

The viscount chuckled. "I see. I regret the somewhat dismal beginning to our acquaintance. Perhaps we should cry pax and start over."

"I confess that would suit me very well. I would like to forget everything that happened this afternoon."

"Everything?" he teased, an amused glint in his slate blue eyes.

The tips of her ears grew warm. "You are incorrigible, sir."

"Better incorrigible than unrepentant. You see? I am improving already."

"An admirable trend. I commend you."

"Then allow me to continue it; this afternoon I found something that I believe belongs to you, and I would like to return it."

Jane's heart lurched sideways in her chest, and she

licked her suddenly dry lips. "And what would that be, my lord?"

"Two somethings, actually—a small book and your shawl. You must have dropped them when the branch collapsed." He frowned. "Are you unwell? You have turned quite pale."

Before she could reply, Lord Langley cupped her elbow and led her away from the crush of dancers. He settled her beside an open set of French doors. "Stay here, and I will fetch you some lemonade."

"Th-thank you," she stammered.

Panic closed around her throat as she watched him wend his way through the crowd toward the refreshment table. He had the List. Oh, sweet heaven . . . Had he read it? He gave no indication of having done so, but even if he had, would he admit it? Her hands grew clammy inside her leather gloves; the cuts and scratches on her fingers stung. Pen was never going to forgive her—

"Drink this." Viscount Langley pressed a cup into her hand.

Jane sipped the lemonade, then made a face; the concoction could do with quite a bit more sugar, but she finished it, bitterness and all. The acrid, lemony tang restored her and unstuck her tongue from the roof of her mouth.

"Thank you, my lord," she said. "I feel a little better now."

His concerned expression eased. "I am relieved to hear it. Would you like to rejoin your mother and sister?"

"No—not yet. Penelope would be alarmed and insist on taking me home immediately. I do not wish to spoil her evening." Jane struggled to keep her voice steady.

"Then perhaps you would like to take a turn about the room and get some air."

She nodded, then took his proffered arm.

"This leaves us with a bit of a problem," he commented.

A tiny frown furrowed her brow. "What do you mean?"

"Had I known you would be here this evening, I might have arranged some discreet way to return your property to you, but now I realize it would not have been as easy as that. Your mother is quite . . . vigilant."

"Yes, she is," Jane agreed with a sigh. Even now she could all but feel Lady Portia's vitriolic gaze drilling into her.

"And doubtless she would be curious if a package were to arrive for you," he speculated.

"She would stand over me while I opened it."

"Despite what you think of me, imp, I do desire to protect your reputation. So—how am I to get these things back to you? Do you have a maid you can trust?"

Jane thought of McBride and gave her head a vehement shake. "No, my lord. We are renting the house for the Season, and I know very little about the servants."

"Then I am at a bit of a loss," he confessed.

"Do you ride, my lord?"

He quirked a golden brown brow at her. "Of course."

"By happy circumstance, so do I. As a matter of fact, I ride every morning in Hyde Park. If we were to encounter each other at the entrance to Rotten Row at, say, eight o'clock, no one would have cause to think anything of it, would they?"

"True. Capital idea." A slow, wicked smile spread over the viscount's handsome face. "No one would ever suspect we have an assignation."

A strange wave of giddiness swept her. "You are impertinent, my lord."

"Impertinent?" His smile broadened. "You have already declared me incorrigible. At this rate, my dear, you will quickly run out of epithets."

Jane smiled, then ducked her head. She was enjoying this too much. "I think I had best return to my sister, my lord."

"As you wish."

They traversed the room, finally arriving at the corner where Penelope stood. Her older sister appeared to be enjoying an animated conversation with Mr. Havelock and Lord Nigel, and she seemed content and more relaxed than she had been in days. Jane's heart soared, hovered, then reversed direction and slid into the soles of her dancing slippers when she realized that their mother would not allow Pen to consider either gentleman as a potential husband.

Lord Langley bent his head toward hers. "I shall look forward to seeing you tomorrow," he murmured.

Jane shivered, suddenly very aware of the viscount's presence—the warmth of his body, the crisp scent of his cologne, the pressure of his hand on hers. She nodded, unable to find her voice.

He bowed, then drifted away, headed for Penelope. Jane watched him go, then drew back when Lady Portia cast a venomous glance in her direction.

She found a vacant chair near the window and perched on the edge of it. She was not usually mistaken in her estimate of a person's character, but it seemed she had misjudged Viscount Langley. Just this afternoon she had promised herself that she would avoid his company; now she found herself looking forward to their meeting tomorrow morning, and not just because she needed to retrieve the List.

What a widgeon! She shook herself. It would not do for her to develop any feelings for Corinthian like him. She had an understanding with Augustus; she could not in good conscience renege on her promise to him. Besides, her mother would be even more incensed if she thought that Jane showed a preference for the viscount's company.

A flash of silver and white caught her eye; she turned to see Penelope speaking with Lord Langley. The viscount must have said something particularly flattering; Pen blushed and hid a smile behind her fan. Jane bit her lip. They certainly made an attractive couple. Could he be the one? He met her sister's criteria: intelligence, wit, amiability, a title. And he was heir to a fortune of his own. If he was half as charming to Pen as he was to her, Pen would be in love with him by the end of the week.

If only her own heart were immune.

"Why so pensive, Sebastian?" Jace asked, and he reached for the bottle of port. "I thought the evening went quite well. You danced twice with Miss Winthrop, and Miss Gray seemed to dote upon your every word. And although you did not manage to secure a dance with Miss Rutledge, she seemed to find you amusing, which is a step in the right direction."

"Amusing is not good enough," Sebastian replied sourly. "I had no idea the girl would be so skittish."

"Then perhaps you should set your sights on an easier pigeon," scoffed Nigel from the chair nearest the fireplace.

The viscount's mouth hardened. "No. Miss Rutledge is perfect."

"You mean her fortune is perfect."

"She is everything I want and more. I simply have to make a greater effort to secure her regard."

Jace refilled his glass, then settled himself on the plush divan. "Her mother made no secret that she approves of you."

"Approves?" Nigel interjected with a snort. "Lud, she way she emptied the butter boat over you, one would think she had you leg-shackled to the girl already."

"If only Miss Rutledge herself shared that same eagerness," the viscount muttered. He paced the floor of Jace's study, swirling the measure of ruby-red port in his glass. Though he had been at his most charming, Miss Rutledge appeared indifferent to him. When he did manage to engage her in conversation, she remained polite but elusive, revealing little about herself. What was she about? He could not even guess where he stood among her other admirers; she showed no particular interest in any one gentleman. Blast.

"What do you plan to do from here?" Jace inquired.

Sebastian heaved a sigh. "I cannot give up just yet. I need something that will make me stand out from her other admirers to break through her reserve, and to do that I need to know more about her."

"Question their servants," Nigel suggested. "Servants always seem to know everything about everyone in the house. They're your neighbors, by Jove. It should not be difficult to get some information."

"If she thinks me too premeditated in my pursuit, she may bolt," Sebastian argued. "I have a better idea. Did you notice that most of Miss Rutledge's admirers ignored her sister? The beauty, I believe, feels those slights most keenly. If I befriend the sister, I gain an ally in my courtship of the beauty."

Jace arched a quizzical brow. "Do you really think that will work?"

"I will know soon enough."

"Well, the sister already seems to think very highly of you," Nigel said, then pulled a face. "Egad, now *there's* an antidote if ever I've seen one. Careful, Sebastian. In my opinion that is the type of female who, overlooked and overshadowed by greater beauty, grows desperate for any scrap of consideration thrown her way. Pay her attention and she'll take to following you around like a faithful spaniel."

"Gammon," Sebastian said with a scowl. "She is no more spaniel-like than you are."

"You do feel pity for her, don't you?" Nigel prodded.

"That is not the point."

"Then I sincerely hope you can tolerate that drab little creature. She possesses little refinement, no distinction of character, and absolutely nothing of beauty to recommend her."

Jace regarded him with disgust. "Is beauty all you care about?"

With a laugh, Nigel leaned back in his chair and propped one foot atop the nearby table. "What else is there?"

"Not all ladies have the good fortune to be beautiful," Havelock riposted, "but they have other admirable qualities. Had you deigned to talk with Miss Jane, you would have found her very amiable, as I did."

"Then perhaps you should take up with her and spare Sebastian the trouble," Nigel sneered.

Jace levered himself from the sofa and stalked to the

sideboard. "One of these days, Nigel, you will discover that women have a very long memory for the casual slights you seem to think amusing and dispense with impunity."

"As if I give a fig for the opinion of such a plain-faced nobody. She is nothing but a little country mouse! Most likely she will end up a spinster or a companion to a nip-cheese dowager who keeps a houseful of incontinent pugs."

Jace glared at him. "Nigel, you're as high on the instep as that brother of yours."

"Thank you."

"I did not mean that as a compliment."

Weary of his friends' bickering, Sebastian set aside his empty glass. "Well, gentlemen, I must be off," he announced.

"So soon? It's barely past midnight," Nigel complained.

"I have an appointment early tomorrow morning," the viscount replied, "one I cannot afford to miss, so I must bid you good evening." Despite their objections, Sebastian sketched a bow and took his leave.

As his carriage rumbled through the darkened streets of Mayfair, Sebastian settled back against the leather squabs, Nigel's warning still ringing through his mind. Did his strategy run the risk of capturing the affections of the wrong woman?

No . . . the imp had her own admirers, he was sure of that now. After he had danced with her, a few other gentlemen followed suit, and she did not lack for partners. Why else would both sisters be in London, if not to find husbands? Then there was her journal. When he mentioned it during their dance, she had lost all color, and though she had feigned nonchalance, only a fool would fail to recognize how important it was to her—and he was no fool. She wanted it back, and quickly. He understood her sense of urgency; if anyone else were to find out, it would embarrass her at best and ruin her reputation at worst.

One other question nagged him. Why did the imp seek only titled beaux? Had no one else struck her fancy enough to merit an entry in the journal? Had their overbearing mother declared that each of her daughters must marry a peer of the realm? That was a possibility, but Jane had no fortune that he was aware of, nor did Lady Portia display the same indulgent regard for her younger daughter as she did for her elder. He had a theory but could not yet determine if it was correct.

He sighed and settled himself more comfortably into one corner of the carriage. In a few hours, if all went well, he would know enough about the Rutledge sisters to make sense of this puzzle.

Chapter Four

Jane touched her heel to her horse's flank and urged him to a canter. Tamerlane responded with a rush of energy that she barely managed to restrain; he wanted to gallop, but proper young ladies did not gallop in Hyde Park, so Jane held him in. The dapple gray tossed his head and tried to take the bit in his teeth, but she remained firm. At last he capitulated with what sounded suspiciously like a snort of equine disgust.

"I quite agree," Jane said under her breath. "It's not Wellbourne, but it must do for now. Come on, old boy."

The lush, misty landscape flashed by as Tam settled into a comfortable, ground-eating stride. Given the overcast skies and the patchy, low-lying fog that hugged the ground, very few other riders occupied the park. All the better.

Jane ducked her head and looked behind to see if Will had managed to keep up with her; the groom lagged behind at a discreet distance. Good. She steered Tamerlane toward Rotten Row.

She leaned forward over the gelding's sleek neck. The wind sang a wild song in her ears, and the rhythmic drumming of Tam's hoofbeats formed a counterpoint.

The fog swirled around them, and she fancied herself soaring like a bird, away from London, away from all the worries that plagued her.

From the moment they left the Symingtons' ball, Lady Portia had hounded Penelope about her seemingly indifferent behavior toward Viscount Langley, especially when Lady Portia had made it clear that she approved of the gentleman. Jane had rushed to Pen's defense, but their mother, in high dudgeon, would hear none of it. She accused her elder daughter of everything from ingratitude to deliberately trying to embarrass the family, and warned that if Pen did not do her duty and bring a lord up to scratch soon, she would lock Pen in her room and arrange a match to the first peer who offered for her, no matter what his age, and that there was nothing Pen could do about it. She went on to ring a peal over Penelope's head for being too particular, too reserved, and too unfeeling of her mother's sensibilities and all the sacrifices she had made on her behalf.

When they reached home, poor Pen, in tears, dashed straight up the stairs to her room. Lady Portia claimed a sick headache and retired to her chamber, refusing to speak to anyone. Jane knocked on Penelope's door to try to comfort her, but Pen did not answer, though Jane could hear her sobbing.

What to do? Only once before had she felt this helpless, and she hated it no less now.

First and foremost, she needed to retrieve the List. Several new candidates, including Lord Langley, had presented themselves at the ball. She needed to convince Pen that her situation was not as desperate as their mother had made it out to be. At least, she hoped she could; never had she seen her sister so distraught as she was last night.

Jane gritted her teeth. Once Lady Portia had made up

her mind, she was as inflexible as a block of marble, and no one had the power to persuade her to reconsider her decision. In the past, Jane, Pen, and their father had been able to find ways to circumvent Lady Portia's unyielding stubbornness, but Jane had the sinking feeling that if she so much as attempted to dissuade her mother from this course of action, she would be packed off to Leicestershire, leaving Penelope in London to fend for herself at the mercy of their single-minded parent.

Her hands tightened on the reins; her mount tossed his head in protest.

"Sorry, Tam," she said. "I am not angry at *you*."

She slowed the horse to a walk, then glanced up at the sky; pale sunlight glowed faintly through the curtain of the clouds overhead. The mist that swirled around Tamerlane's hooves would soon begin to dissipate, as would the damp chill in the air.

As she approached Rotten Row, the gelding lifted his head and smelled the air, nostrils flared. A man astride a chestnut mare appeared from behind a stand of trees. Jane recognized Viscount Langley instantly; he cut a very fine figure in his Egyptian brown jacket and buckskin breeches.

"Good morning, imp," he greeted her. He tipped his hat, then squinted up at the sky and gave a lopsided grin. "Such lovely weather you've arranged for us."

Jane wheeled Tamerlane around so the two horses stood abreast. "Good morning, my lord." She did not return his smile.

His merriment faded. "Is something wrong?"

"Nothing of importance," she replied hastily. "Did you bring the—my property?"

The viscount glanced past her to her groom, who remained a respectful distance away. "Can your man be trusted to be discreet?"

Jane followed his gaze, then nodded. "I have known Will since I was a girl. I trust him implicitly."

"Good." He reached into the leather pouch behind his saddle, then handed her a neat bundle wrapped in paper. "I believe this is what you were looking for."

Jane tore one corner of the paper to see a patch of her periwinkle-colored wool shawl. She could feel the hard outline of the List within its folds; the tension in her neck and shoulders eased. "Thank you, my lord." She quickly tucked the packet into the oversize reticule she had slung over her saddle bow, then rearranged her skirts to cover it.

"You seem troubled," he persisted. "If you'll pardon me for saying so, imp, you look as though you did not sleep a wink all night."

Jane seized her lower lip between her teeth. She desperately wanted to confide in someone; she had held so much inside for so long. The viscount had been so kind to her last night—dare she trust him?

He gestured with his riding crop. "The fog will not lift for some time yet, I think. Let us ride a while together."

She wavered.

"Unless, of course, you need to return home," he added.

She thought about the oppressive silence that reigned over their rented town house, then shook her head. "No . . . I have no pressing engagements."

"I understand if you do not wish to reveal the cause of your distress," he began, "but I entreat you to look upon me as a friend. I suspect you are in need of one."

"My mother would tell me that ladies do not form

friendships with gentlemen," Jane replied, unable to keep the bitterness from her voice.

Again that appealing, lopsided grin. "But you have stated before that I am no gentleman, so I believe you are safe on that account."

"You delight in teasing me."

"I do, but only because you need teasing. Why, you barely smiled at all last night. You are too young to be so somber and serious all the time. How old are you? Seventeen? Eighteen?"

"I shall be nineteen this autumn."

"There, you see? When I was eighteen I had not a care in the world."

"If only I could be so fortunate," Jane murmured.

"I beg your pardon?"

"Do you have family, my lord?" she asked suddenly.

Lord Langley's face went blank. "There is only my father, the Earl of Stanhope. My mother died when I was very young."

"No brothers or sisters?"

A muscle twitched in his jaw. "One brother. Alexander—Alex."

She recognized the name. "Ah . . . you were conversing with him in the garden yesterday, weren't you?"

"You were eavesdropping," he accused.

"I did not make a point of it," she replied. "But I could hear you quite well from my side of the wall."

The viscount rubbed the back of his neck. "Yes, I suppose I was speaking to Alex, in a way. He has been dead for the last five years. The house used to belong to him."

She gasped. "I am so sorry. Was he—was he with the army in the Peninsula?"

"No. Alex's death was the most singular piece of idiocy . . ." He stopped himself, then exhaled in a long, controlled sigh. "My father had summoned him home for Christmas, even though the weather had rendered the roads nigh unto impassable. Alex was traveling through a snowstorm when the carriage broke an axle and over-turned. The coachman was killed; my brother suffered a broken back and could not move. No one found him until a few days later. By then he was dead."

Jane's eyes rounded in shock. "How terrible," she breathed. "Why would your father insist that he travel in such weather?"

"Because my father is a tyrant." Lord Langley's voice quivered with anger. He paused a moment and composed himself. "Forgive me. I presume too much familiarity."

"You need not apologize, my lord; I understand your anger. You blame your father for your brother's death."

"I do, and I have made no secret of it."

"We have more in common than one might think; your father sounds very much like my mother."

His lips quirked in a faint, sardonic smile. "With one possible exception: my father does not breathe fire. He prefers to ignore me."

"Then I envy you. If my mother had enough sense to do the same, I would be the happiest girl in the world." Jane clapped a hand over her mouth. "I should not have said that."

The viscount chuckled. "You little hypocrite. It's all right to think such things, but God forbid you should ac-tually say them."

She pulled a face at him.

"I take it your mother is the cause of your blue devils?" he asked. Then, more softly, "Did something happen last night?"

Jane sighed. "No, nothing happened, and that is pre-cisely the problem."

"Indeed?"

"My mother has decided that my sister must marry a peer," she explained. "Preferably an earl or a marquess." She glanced sideways at him. "Although she has not ruled out viscounts, especially those who are heirs to earldoms."

"So I gathered," he drawled. "And . . . ?"

"And Pen is not making her choice fast enough to please my mother."

"Penelope choosing from among her suitors," murmured Lord Langley. "An irony of mythical proportions. But the Season has just begun. Surely Lady Portia does not wish your sister to make a hasty decision, one she might later regret."

"Then you do not know my mother. I have a theory, my lord. I believe she wishes my sister to marry well because she herself could not. If Pen makes a brilliant match at the beginning of the Season, Mama can crow about it to everyone who snubbed her in the past. If my sister refuses too many offers or takes too long to make her choice, my mother will feel humiliated."

"A cork-brained notion if ever I heard one," he muttered.

"Last night she berated Pen mercilessly because she did not encourage your attentions—or those of any of her other illustrious admirers, for that matter."

"I assume your sister has a reason for doing so."

"Of course she does!" Jane exclaimed. "She cannot choose a husband on the merit of his title alone. She is entitled to know something of a man's character before she accepts his proposal of marriage. One dance does not constitute grounds for an engagement."

"Very sensible of her," he replied. "I take it Lady Portia does not see the wisdom of this approach."

"No. And it does not help that Pen is shy of strangers. You seem surprised, my lord. Had you not noticed her reticence?"

"Yes, but I merely thought her unreceptive to my charm."

"My sister would like to take her time and make a prudent match, but Mama is growing impatient. Let me put it to you this way, my lord. My mother wanted her to accept the Earl of Haydon simply on the basis of his rank."

"Haydon?" Lord Langley's brows rose in surprise. "That old reprobate? The man's a loose screw if ever there was one."

"Which is precisely why my sister refused him. Mama was most displeased. And when she is displeased . . . My mother has quite a temper, my lord, and can be very cruel when she wishes to be. But last night—last night she was in rare form. Pen took to her bed in tears."

"Poor creature. Is there anything I can do to help you cheer her up?"

Jane eyed him speculatively. Did he ask out of genuine concern or because he wanted to win Pen's favor? "What did you have in mind?"

"Is she fond of any particular sort of sweet? Ices, perhaps? Or flowers?"

"Every day her other admirers send so many posies that every flower shop and greenhouse in London must be stripped bare. And Pen has never been one for sweets—anything with almonds in it, especially marzipan, gives her a dreadful rash. But she likes Spanish oranges very much."

"Do you think such an offering would please her?"

"It might."

"Then I will see to it immediately. I sympathize with your sister; I know what it's like to be the object of a parent's unrelenting censure." He cocked his head. "What about you, imp?"

She started. "Me?"

"What sort of offerings please you?"

"You are teasing me again, my lord."

"Not at all. You mentioned the trinkets your sister receives, but what do your admirers send you?"

"My admirers?" she echoed. All she could think of was Augustus Wingate's trout-like countenance. "I don't—that is . . ."

He stared at her for a moment. His eyes narrowed. "The book does not belong to you, does it?"

"Why do you say that?" She clutched at the reins as a wave of coldness swept over her.

"If it did, I suspect you would readily admit to being courted by the gentlemen whose names are listed therein."

"What—?" Jane's heart pounded wildly within the prison of her chest. "You had no right to read it—how dare you!"

The viscount had the good grace to look ashamed. "I do apologize. I opened it thinking it was yours, that it would provide me with your name, since you would not."

Tamerlane snorted and tossed his head until Jane loosened her grip. "Your noble intentions give me little consolation, my lord," she fumed. He knew. *He knew!*

"I assure you I did not make the connection until now. The names in the book, the fact that your sister must marry a peer, her thoughtful, deliberate manner, and— forgive me—your own lack of visible beaux."

Jane's blush scalded her skin all the way to her hairline.

"So I must conclude that the book belongs to your sister. How did it come into your possession?"

Jane's head snapped up. "I did not steal it."

"I never said you did."

"My sister feared our mother would find out about it, so she entrusted it to me. And I lost it. And now you know, and everything is ruined!"

He held up a hand. "Calm yourself. Your secret — and hers — is safe with me. I have no wish to embarrass either of you."

She glared at him. "Will you promise me that you will never speak of this to my sister?"

"I give you my word of honor. You love your sister and would do anything for her. I envy you that."

She blinked. "You do?"

"I have seen too many families torn apart by jealousy or favoritism," Lord Langley said grimly, "including my own."

"You and your brother?"

"Yes. Alex and I were never allowed to be close. When I think about how many years I wasted hating him, wanting to be like him, I —" He broke off, then shifted in the saddle.

"I am sorry, my lord," she said softly.

A look of pain distorted his handsome features. "Go home to your sister, Miss Jane. Go home, and put your mind at ease."

"Thank you." Jane swallowed around the lump in her throat "I — I was wrong about you, my lord. You are indeed a gentleman."

She turned her mount and rode off. Sebastian watched as she and her gray gelding disappeared into the mist, her groom trailing behind. A fey girl on her fey mount . . . He shook himself. Egad, when had he become prone to such ridiculous flights of fancy? He nudged his mare with his knees and headed for the park gate.

Imagination or not, astride that long-legged gray, in a close-fitting habit of spruce green wool that turned her huge eyes the color of lichen, Jane Rutledge had looked more like an elfin creature than ever this morning. And where had she learned to ride like that? Few females of Sebastian's acquaintance could handle a horse of that size with such ease.

What he found even more odd was the fact that she inspired such trust. It was not like him to share a confidence on the spur of the moment, yet he had told her about Alex. He had never revealed so much of himself to anyone but Nigel and Jace, and he had known them for years. And now he had just imparted something of his own private hell to her. What the devil had come over him?

If only she were an heiress. The viscount smiled ruefully. Another flight of fancy. While he held a certain fondness for her, they would never rub along well together, and she certainly would never accept the sort of marriage he was after. To accomplish that he needed a sweet, docile wife, and Miss Jane was anything but docile. He needed to concentrate less on teasing her and more on winning her sister's hand.

Sebastian thoughts returned to the mysterious book. He had every intention of keeping the imp's secret, but that did not mean he couldn't use the information to his own advantage. He had not been impressed with the fellows whose names were written in it; neither, apparently, had Miss Rutledge. She seemed a sensible sort of girl, one who was impressed more with good conversation than immense quantities of flowers or fatuous odes to her eyebrows. Thank God he had never been one for poetry; he would be in dire straits if he needed to start spouting it now!

From what she had written, he surmised that Miss Rutledge desired a specific sort of gentleman as a husband, a man who was intelligent, sensitive, charming, witty, and not after her fortune. He could be all that and never let on that he needed her twenty-five thousand pounds; after they were married, she wouldn't need to know what became of her dowry—nor would he have to tell her, if he was discreet enough.

All he had to do was pierce the armor of her shyness. And, thanks to Jane, he knew just where to begin. He spurred his mare into a trot; he had arrangements to make.

"Pen?" Jane rapped on her sister's chamber door. "Are you all right? You did not come down for nuncheon, and I'm worried about you."

No answer.

She knocked again. "I know you are in there, Pen. Please open the door."

After the span of several heartbeats, the door opened a crack. Penelope's drawn face appeared in the opening. "Come in, dearest," she murmured.

Jane slipped into the room and hugged her sister. "Are you well?" she inquired anxiously, surveying Pen's pale cheeks and reddened eyes.

Her sister nodded, then closed her chamber door. She meandered over to the set of Chippendale chairs by the window and perched upon one of them. With a listless hand she picked up her embroidery hoop from the nearby table, then set it aside again. "As well as can be expected," she replied dully. "Did Mama send you?"

Jane lowered herself into the chair opposite her. "Oh, come now, you know better than that. I *was* worried. You are never melancholy for this long."

"I suppose there is a first time for everything."

Jane reached out and took one of Pen's hands in her own. "Do not allow Mama to vex you. You must do what you think is best."

Pen pulled away. "I do not know what that is anymore." She drew a wrinkled handkerchief from her cuff and pressed it to her tear-filled eyes. "Why do I even bother? I will only end up as the wife of a man old enough to be my grandfather."

Jane steeled herself, then took a deep breath. "Stop this at once, Penelope Catherine Rutledge. A good cry is one thing, but now you are feeling sorry for yourself, and it serves no purpose at all."

"What would you have me do?" Pen demanded, her lower lip quivering. She slumped back in her chair. "Mama finds fault with everything. I can do nothing right."

"Rubbish. Now stop being such a blancmange and listen. How many gentlemen did you meet last night at the ball?"

A slight frown creased Penelope's forehead. "I am not certain. Twenty, perhaps. Or thirty. There were so many."

"Very well, let us say thirty, then. And of those thirty, how many meet Mama's requirements?"

"You mean, how many have a title," Pen sulked, wrapping her arms around her body. "The sole measure of a man's worth. Never mind kindness or intelligence or character."

"Well, how many?" Jane persisted.

Pen sighed. "About half, I should say."

"Excellent. And how many of those gentlemen made a favorable impression on you?"

Her sister sat up. "What are you getting at, dearest?"

"Answer the question."

Penelope appeared to make a quick mental tally. "Six or seven."

"How many of those gentlemen would you like to see again?"

"All of them, I suppose. Jane, what—"

Jane thrust the List into her sister's hands. "Well, then, there is hope, is there not? If you do not wish to see yourself wed to a seventy-year-old roué with false teeth and a creaking corset, then it is up to you to do something about it. You cannot mope about all day; if you lie about and do nothing, Mama is sure to take matters into her own hands, and neither of us wants that."

"No—you are right." Pen straightened and opened the book.

"Now . . . who comes to mind first?" Jane prompted.

Penelope removed the pencil from its loop. "What about Viscount Langley?"

Jane tried to ignore the way her heart turned over at the mention of his name. "All right—what about him?"

"I hope you are not cross with me for asking him to dance with you."

"No—as long as it does not happen too often. I know what you were up to, Pen, and it won't fadge. I am not interested in these London fribbles." Jane crossed her fingers and hid them in the folds of her skirt. "You must think about yourself for a change."

"Dearest, I—"

Jane shook her head. "What did you think of him?"

"Oh . . . yes." Pen scribbled a few lines in the book. "I admit I was hesitant at first, remembering how Mama had sung his praises without having the slightest knowledge of his character. She had done the same with the Earl of Haydon, and we both know how *he* turned out. But upon closer examination, I must say I thought the viscount very handsome and cordial. Still, he danced with you only once."

"Penelope." Jane forced her voice to remain level. "If you are going to judge the worth of your admirers, do so on how many times they wish to dance with *you*, not with me."

Her sister flushed. "Yes, but I will not give any thought to a man who slights you because you are not as — as — well . . ."

Jane rolled her eyes. "Oh, for pity's sake, stop this roundaboutation and say it. Because I am not as beautiful as you are. I do not begrudge you your looks, Pen. I never have. Not everyone can be a diamond of the first water — it would lessen their value. But I comprehend your meaning. Anyone who sees only beauty is not worth having."

Pen nodded. "Quite right. So far he appears rather promising. What about you? What is your opinion of him?"

Jane shifted a bit on her chair. "I found him — I found him not at all what I expected."

"How so?"

"Well, given the gossip we have heard, I thought he would be an unrepentant rakehell —"

"Jane!"

"Well, I did."

Her eyes widened. "And is he?"

"No. Not at all. He is merely — incorrigible."

Pen frowned. "You are speaking in riddles, dearest."

Jane nearly bit her tongue at the slip. "What I mean to say is that his wit may be wicked, and he may try a bit too hard to be charming, but he has a kind heart. He might bear closer consideration."

"Does the 'wicked wit' fall under Merits or Drawbacks?" Pen glanced up from her writing.

"Both."

Penelope finished with a flourish. "Done." Then she hesitated, pencil poised. "As long as we are on the subject of Lord Langley, what do you think of his friends?"

"Why do you ask? We cannot add them to the List, for neither has a title."

Pen lowered her eyes. "True, but some say you can judge a man by the company he keeps."

"If that is the case, what does that say about the viscount? His friends are — well — singular individuals. Take Lord Nigel, for example."

"You do not like him?"

Jane wrinkled her nose. "He is a vain, toplofty peacock. And no, I do not like him. The other one, though, the dark-haired gentleman — what was his name?"

"Mr. Havelock."

"He seemed quite kind. And he is very amiable. I noticed you spoke with him at length last night."

"He owns a fleet of ships and has recently been to the West Indies. He was telling me tales of all the exotic places to which he has traveled."

"He is in trade?" Jane frowned. A duke's younger brother and a shipowner — how did Lord Langley come to make such dissimilar acquaintances? "Careful, Pen. Mama will box your ears if she learns you've been hobnobbing with a Cit."

Her sister lifted one shoulder in a negligent shrug. "He is Lord Langley's friend, so I did not believe she would object too much. Besides, I found his conversation most diverting, which is more than I can say for some of the other gentlemen present. Speaking of whom . . . about the Earl of Wychford . . ."

Another hour passed before they finished updating the List to Penelope's satisfaction. With that accomplished,

Jane rose, stretched, and smoothed a few errant locks of hair away from her eyes.

"Well, Pen?" she asked. "Was I right? Is the situation not nearly as bleak as you imagined?"

Penelope closed the journal. "Yes, you were right, dearest, but you need not look so smug about it."

Jane made no effort to conceal her grin. "Then tell me—who is your most likely prospect?"

"Though it may astound you, I have to say Viscount Langley. Can you believe it? After Mama went to such lengths to recommend him to me, and I went to such lengths to avoid him because of it! When I meet him next, for I am certain I will, I might even encourage him." Amusement glinted in her green eyes.

"Mama will be ecstatic," Jane drawled.

"Ecstatic? She will want to dash out and buy my wedding clothes this very minute!"

The two of them giggled and chattered away like schoolgirls until McBride rapped at the chamber door. At the sound of the dresser's voice, Pen jumped up from her chair and tucked the List beneath her mattress.

"In a moment," she called.

Jane gathered herself to leave, and Penelope whispered, "Thank you, dearest. I do not know what I should do without you."

Jane smiled. "Well, I could not stand by and watch you fret and moan and wring your hands like one of the featherheaded heroines in those Minerva Press novels of yours. You would drive us both mad."

Pen's eyes sparkled. "Do you suppose we will see Lord Langley tonight?"

"I should be very surprised if we did not. I would not put it past Mama to have sent him a schedule of our social activities."

Penelope stifled a laugh. "Then I shall have to remember to act surprised."

Heartened by the cheerfulness in her sister's voice, Jane excused herself and crossed the hall to her own room. McBride would attend to Lady Portia first, then to Penelope, then to her last of all, which left her a brief period of welcome solitude before they resumed their social whirlwind.

She went to the window that overlooked the garden and gazed down at the neatly laid out patterns of blooms and greenery. She should not be so surprised that Pen favored Viscount Langley over the other bachelors on the List; he was everything Penelope desired in a husband. And with her beauty and sweetness, Pen was certainly everything the viscount could desire in a wife.

At last her sister had found a gentleman who seemed to appreciate her for who she was, rather than for her twenty-five thousand pounds. A gentleman who could very well steal her heart. A gentleman who would adore and protect her for the rest of her life.

She was thrilled for Pen, truly she was. But why, beneath the happiness, did she feel so empty?

Sebastian sauntered through the front door of his town house, whistling, and handed his hat and gloves to a startled footman. Who would have thought a few days would make such a difference? He was making progress with the beauteous Penelope at last; her green eyes had sparkled with pleasure when he'd presented her with a wrapped box of Valencia oranges and another of hothouse strawberries. She had agreed to go driving with him in Hyde Park. She had even danced with him.

In fact, he had made so much progress that he decided the time had come to make a more daring move: just a few hours ago, at the Peterboroughs' ball, he had waltzed Miss Rutledge out onto an empty, shadowed balcony and kissed her.

As kisses went, it was not the most stellar of his career, but it had been a start. Miss Rutledge had held perfectly still, her lips soft and pliant beneath his. Other than a slight catch in her breath, however, she did not react at all. He may as well have bussed a marble statue. But she had not pulled away from him or balked in any way. When he pulled his head back, she had looked up at him, a surprised expression on her beautiful face, and said, "That was—nice."

Nice? He had been as tender and gentle as he could so as not to frighten her, but—nice? He would rather face down a French firing squad than have his kisses described in such a tepid manner. Passionate, dizzying, intoxicating, yes—*nice* was not in his repertoire. Usually. She appeared to enjoy it, though, so he would settle for that. For now, at least.

One person, however, had not thought him nice at all.

Once he had returned Miss Rutledge to her mother, Jace had dragged him aside, his expression stormy.

"What did you do to her?" Havelock demanded.

"I beg your pardon?" Sebastian asked, puzzled. Rarely was his even tempered friend so snappish. "Do to whom?"

"You known damn well to whom. To Miss Rutledge! You disappeared out onto the balcony with her, then brought her back with her face flushed and her gown rumpled."

"I had no idea you had been observing us so closely," the viscount drawled.

His friend reddened. "I was watching your back, Sebastian. Someone had to, obviously."

"Cut line, Jace. All I did was kiss her."

"You kissed her?" Havelock repeated in outraged tones.

"Yes. Is that so extraordinary?"

"Do you care nothing for the lady's reputation? What if someone saw you? You could have ruined her."

"Devil take it, man, lower your voice," Sebastian said with a low growl.

Havelock seemed to collect himself, but the line of his jaw remained taut. "Or was that your strategy from the start?"

The viscount's eyes narrowed. "What are you implying?"

"Did you intend to compromise the lady so that she will have to marry you?"

Sebastian folded his arms over his chest. "I am not so desperate that I would resort to such villainy, and you know it."

"Oh, really?" Havelock did not look convinced in the least.

"What is this all about, Jace?"

"She's a sweet young lady, Sebastian. I do not wish to see her hurt."

"Hurt?" The viscount peered at his friend as though the man had sprouted feathers. "I am not going to hurt her, Jace. I need her. Or, rather, I need her blunt."

"Just don't do anything you might regret," Havelock muttered, then stalked off through the crowd.

Hours later, this scene still preyed on Sebastian's mind. He walked down the hall to Alex's study—*his* study—and poured himself a glass of port. It was unlike Jace to behave so strangely. What had gotten into him? He had sounded almost—jealous. Had he formed a *tendre* for the lady? The viscount shook his head. Lady Por-

tia had mandated that Miss Rutledge marry a peer, which
left Jace out of the running.

Sebastian sipped at his drink. Once the lovely Penelope had been removed from the Marriage Mart, perhaps
his friend would consider paying court to Jane, instead.
He frowned. Havelock and Jane were level headed, admirable people, but somehow the thought of his solemn
little imp with Jace made him uneasy. In fact, the thought
of her with anyone made him uneasy. Why?

He shook himself. He would not think about it now; he
must concentrate on his courtship of Miss Rutledge. All
he had to do was survive a few more evenings' worth of
tedious Society functions, for on Thursday next he was
engaged to escort the Rutledge ladies to Vauxhall, where,
if everything went as planned, he would sweep Miss Rutledge off her feet and ask her to marry him in a way she
could not possibly refuse. His smile melded with the rim
of his glass. She did not know it yet, but she was in for
the surprise of her life.

Chapter Five

Despite Penelope's breezy assurances to the contrary, Jane could not rid herself of the notion that something was troubling her sister.

To begin with, over the past few days Pen had begun to act in a very un-Penelope-like manner. Although in public nothing seemed amiss, at home her sister's attention wandered; she seemed preoccupied even in the midst of conversation. She tended to gaze off into space, her gaze dull and clouded. She left her needlework in the oddest places; more than once Jane discovered Pen's embroidery hoop resting on the music stand of the pianoforte or on one of the bookshelves in the library. She had not mentioned adding any new entries to the List—in fact, she had stopped talking about it altogether. Yet, whenever Jane tried to speak with her about the cause of her distraction, Pen merely brightened, smiled, and insisted that nothing was wrong.

What had brought about these odd starts? It was not like Pen to brood or succumb to fits of melancholy. Something had happened—but what?

Pen had been fine up until the night of the Peterboroughs' ball. Whatever had upset her sister, it had occurred that evening. Jane pressed her fingertips to her temples and tried to remember everything that had transpired during the course of that night.

Heartened by their discussion of the List, Penelope had gone to great lengths to overcome her shyness around Lord Langley; she had even agreed to waltz with him. Jane had watched her sister float past in the arms of the handsome viscount, her face aglow with such pleasure that Jane's own heart gave a suspicious twinge. Then the couple had whirled around to the far side of the ballroom floor, out of sight, and the dance ended soon thereafter.

When the viscount brought Pen back to Lady Portia's side, her sister's cheeks were flushed as though she had dashed headlong up a flight of stairs. Lady Portia had been too caught up in conversation with Lord Nigel to notice, but Jane had. Pen did not say a word in response to Jane's questioning look. Strange. Even stranger was the fact that Jason Havelock appeared soon thereafter, his face taut with anger, and drew Lord Langley aside. Although Jane could not hear any of the conversation, she could see from their expressions that the exchange had not been a pleasant one.

Later that evening, Jane observed Pen taking a turn about the room with Mr. Havelock. Her sister regarded the young man with rapt attention, as though fascinated by his every word. Then they had stopped. Mr. Havelock kissed Penelope's fingers—it seemed to Jane that he held her hand a trifle too long for propriety—and her sister ducked her head, a fiery blush rising in her cheeks. At that moment Lady Portia ordered Jane to fetch her a glass of lemonade; although Lord Nigel volunteered to get it for her, Lady Portia remained adamant. Jane hastened to comply, but the distraction caused her to lose sight of Pen and Mr. Havelock.

She returned with the lemonade to find Penelope at their mother's side, her lips slightly swollen, her eyes glazed. Before Jane could ask what had happened, another gentleman claimed her sister for a country dance.

Jane had given the incident little thought at the time, but the more she thought about it, the more questions began to crowd her mind. Had Penelope quarreled with the viscount? What had Lord Langley done to provoke Mr. Havelock's anger? And what had Mr. Havelock said to Pen to make her blush so? Jane recalled the intent expression with which her sister had regarded the young man. Did Pen nurture a secret affection for him? Surely she knew that such a *tendre* was futile; their mother would never allow her to consider a match with a mere mister, much less a Cit, no matter how handsome, how rich, or how amiable the gentleman. Or was she reading far too much into all of this in the first place?

Jane remained uncertain, for Penelope still refused to acknowledge that anything troubled her. She could not in good conscience plague her sister with questions—Lady Portia did that quite well already. Still, it was unlike Pen to remain so tight-lipped. By the time they needed to dress for their evening at Vauxhall, the tension in the house had flayed Jane's nerves to shreds.

As had been her habit of late, Jane sat quietly in her sister's room while McBride laid out Penelope's clothing and arranged her hair. Then the abigail departed to assist Lady Portia, leaving Jane to help her sister dress. Pen took one look at the gown set out for her, scowled, and with a militant expression began to ransack her wardrobe.

Jane looked up from her book and sighed. "Honestly, Pen, will you stop fussing? It hardly matters what you wear; you would look lovely in a burlap bag."

Penelope took another frock from the clothespress and stood in front of her pier glass with it, holding it up against her body. She made a face and tossed the frothy tulle creation onto the bed, where it landed in a careless heap atop the others. "I refuse to wear another insipid white ball gown. I am sick to death of white!"

Jane arched an eyebrow at the rapidly growing mound of fabric. "Mama seems to choose little else for you."

"Of course—she wants me to appear angelic." Pen eyed a dress of white muslin trimmed with silver spangles, then cast it aside. "I have worn white to nearly every ball and party since we've come to London. I am beginning to resemble a ghost, not an angel."

The uncharacteristic petulance in her sister's voice set off another warning in Jane's head. "I wish you would tell me what is bothering you, Pen."

Penelope paused, then made a great show of rummaging through the remaining gowns. "Nothing is wrong, dearest."

"So you keep telling me, but I know you too well to believe it. You have been acting strangely ever since the Peterboroughs' ball."

Pen turned, her green eyes wary. "Have I? I—I cannot fathom your meaning."

"Well, you barely eat anything at breakfast, you seem preoccupied, and I have never known you to be this particular about your appearance. Did something happen between you and the viscount? Have you quarreled?"

Penelope caught her lower lip in her teeth. "Oh, Jane—how can I begin to tell you?"

"Something *did* happen." Jane closed her book with a snap and edged forward in her seat, a frown of concern pulling at her brow. "You can tell me, Pen. Out with it."

Her sister shot a guarded glance toward her chamber door.

"Mama is still at her toilette, which means McBride is with her," Jane said. "We should have no fear of interruption for at least another half hour."

Penelope hesitated.

"Well?"

"He kissed me," Pen blurted, then ducked her head, abashed.

"Viscount Langley?"

"No, the Prince Regent," Pen retorted crossly. "Of course Viscount Langley."

"Oh." A numb sensation began in Jane's chest. "What—what was it like?"

"Well, it was not unpleasant."

"Glowing praise, indeed."

Pen blushed a very vivid pink. "That is to say, it was rather nice. I think I enjoyed it."

"You *think?*" Jane echoed, dubious.

"All right. I did enjoy it."

"Then why are you so ill at ease? You like Lord Langley, do you not?"

"Well—yes."

"If you do not wish to confide in me, Pen," Jane said gently, "I shall not insist upon it."

Guilt shadowed her sister's eyes. "It is not that, dearest."

Jane waited as Penelope paced to the window,

twisted her fingers together, then paced back to the clothespress.

"I believe he is going to declare himself tonight at Vauxhall," Pen declared at length.

The void beneath Jane's breastbone yawned wider. "That—that is wonderful news."

"Yes, I suppose it is."

"You seem uncertain."

"How can I be certain of anything?" Penelope wailed. "The viscount appears to be all I desire in a husband, but our acquaintance spans but a handful of days." She nibbled at the tip of one thumb. "I know so little about him, and the gossip . . ."

Here, then, lay the explanation for her sister's unease. Jane forced her lips into a semblance of a smile. "You have seen as well as I the lengths to which the London tabbies will go to possess the latest *on dit*. Half of everything we hear is outrageous enough to qualify as pure fiction. If you have any doubts, then ask Lord Langley himself about his past. Do not rely on what anyone else tells you, even me."

"What if I do not have the chance before he proposes? If I refuse him, Mama will never forgive me. I—I do not know what to do."

Jane set aside her book, then rose and took her sister's hands. "Pen, I know you pride yourself on your diligence and practicality, but at some point you must put the List away and follow your own heart."

"Do you mean that?" Penelope's question emerged as more of a whisper.

"Of course I do," Jane replied. "All the lists in the world signify nothing if you disregard your own feelings. If you believe he will make you happy, then you should accept him. And I do so want you to be happy."

"Oh, Jane." Pen enveloped her in an impulsive hug. "Thank you. You have ever been the voice of reason."

"In this family, someone has to be," Jane replied with an impudent grin. She gently set Penelope away from her. "Now stop worrying; you will give yourself wrinkles. And then, of course, no one will have you."

"Wretched creature." Pen wrinkled her little retroussé nose, then reluctantly surveyed the heap of gowns on her bed. "That still leaves me in a quandary about which gown to choose."

"Oh, so now we are back to discussing serious matters," Jane teased.

"I am in earnest, dearest. What do I wear? I have never been proposed to before."

"Neither have I—not really, at any rate, so I fear I shall be of little help."

"Then what are *you* wearing?"

"I? The pink faille, I suppose."

"But you wore that to the opera three nights ago."

Jane shrugged. "I see no reason not to wear it again. The pink faille is my favorite; it will do."

"Dearest, why are you always content to play the role of the country mouse?"

Jane started. Pen usually did not say such things. "Because I *am* a country mouse, Pen. I have never aspired to be anything else."

"And that is your problem. Here." Penelope rummaged around in the pile of clothing on the bed and pulled forth a gown of white gossamer satin trimmed with pale pink rosebuds. "This will become you very well."

"Pen, I am not going to wear your dress," Jane objected.

"Why? What are you afraid of—that others might notice you?"

Uncomfortable heat singed Jane's face. "No, of course not."

"Then why not? We are almost of a size. You are a bit more slender through the waist, but we can take in the sides with a few quick stitches."

Eyes wide, Jane stared first at her sister, then at the lovely, ethereal dress. "What has brought this on?"

"I have been such a gudgeon these past few days, and you have been so sweet to me. This is the only way I have to repay you."

Jane looked at the dress again; she had nothing so fine in her own wardrobe. The viscount might even think her pretty. . . . No. She shook herself. Ever since their ride in Hyde Park, Lord Langley had treated her with the amused tolerance one reserved for a younger sister. That was just as well; soon he would be her brother-in-law. She needed to banish these silly romantic notions once and for all. She must.

"I will brook no refusal." A mischievous grin curved Pen's full lips. "We shall both wear white, and the gentlemen will think we are angels fallen from heaven."

Jane threw up her hands. "All right. I can see you are determined to have your way in this."

"I am. And Mama cannot do or say anything to dissuade me."

Not that their mother did not make the attempt. As soon as she and Penelope descended the stairs to the vestibule Jane could see the storm clouds gathering on her mother's brow. She knew the signs well; to say that Lady Portia was displeased was an understatement. With a frigid gaze her mother surveyed Jane from head to toe, her mouth settled into lines of grim disapproval.

Jane tensed, fully expecting Lady Portia to order her back upstairs to change, but to her shock she did not—no doubt due to the presence of Lord Langley, who at that moment arrived to escort them to Vauxhall.

"You look different tonight, Miss Jane," he commented as he assisted her into the carriage. Nothing more than that. Then he turned his attention to Penelope, and soon the equipage rumbled off through the darkened streets.

Jane fidgeted against the plush squabs and tried not to stare at the way the viscount held Penelope's gloved hand in his, the way he caressed her sister's long, slender fingers. She tried to imagine Augustus performing such an intimate gesture, then banished the image. Augustus had held her hand only once, when he had asked if she would consider marriage to him. His clammy clasp had made her shiver then, and she shivered now at the memory.

This was madness!

Watching Pen and Lord Langley, she realized what she wanted.

Love.

The viscount had been right—she was a hypocrite. She might lecture herself about the impracticality of love, but she realized that in her heart she craved that very thing. To be wanted. Adored. Cherished. To have a man gaze at her the way Viscount Langley gazed at Pen.

Jane recognized the intoxicating flattery inherent in that sort of fairy tale—of being swept off one's feet by a handsome prince and living happily ever after. But even though her heart was swayed by such arguments, she must not allow her head to follow suit. She had too many obligations; she needed to hold herself aloof.

Yes, she must be reasonable. As much as she might want to be loved by a handsome, passionate man, what happened once the first blush faded from the rose? Love was a fickle emotion, and a frail one. It might conquer all, as Virgil claimed, but she was not so naïve as to think it was all a marriage needed to succeed; love alone could not endure misfortune and hardship and disappointment. She would never forget what had happened to her father. Wellbourne still paid the price.

Had her mother felt even the smallest measure of love for her spouse? Jane had no way of knowing. Clearly her parents' marriage had suffered from an imbalance of affection. She bit her lip. She could not imagine anything more horrible—to love earnestly and deeply and be treated with indifference in return. Even outright hatred would be preferable to that.

Every shred of sense she possessed told her that love was a luxury she could ill afford. Then why did she still want it so badly?

As with everything one could not have, it grew all the more attractive the more unattainable it became. That had to be it.

Jane rubbed at her temples; all these rational perambulations made her head ache. She fixed her gaze out the carriage window, watching as the street lamps flashed by, pinpoints of light in the darkness. Pen and Lady Portia laughed at one of the viscount's witticisms; Jane flinched at the sound. This would never do. She must not spoil Pen's evening with this bout of selfish melancholy. Pasting a smile on her face, she allowed herself to be drawn into the conversation.

In their supper box, Sebastian looked over the rim of his wineglass at Jane. He need not have worried that she would notice his surreptitious glances; she kept her gaze fixed anywhere but on him—on Penelope, on his friends, on the crowd gathered in the Grove, or on her plate, though she had hardly touched any of the chicken, pigeon pie, muslin-thin slices of ham, or other delicacies set before her. Delicacies that cost him a small fortune, but he would not think about that tonight.

Something troubled her. Her eyes had turned the color of tarnished pewter, and her skin seemed to draw taut around her mouth. He had seen the same signs during their meeting in Hyde Park. Surely she could not be upset with anything he had done; he had been a pattern-card of propriety these past few days. When he brought gifts to Penelope, he brought smaller offerings for Jane and Lady Portia. He had escorted them around Town and taken assiduous care that the imp not feel left out. So what was the matter with her?

By contrast, Penelope fairly glowed with excitement and spoke in an animated manner with everyone. Her glossy black ringlets danced with every movement; it was all he could do to keep from reaching out to twine one of those curls around his finger. Later, he promised himself.

At his other side, Lady Portia chatted with Nigel—rather, she chattered *at* him. Nigel's dazzling smile showed signs of strain around the edges. Sebastian suspected he would owe his friend a very great debt when this business was over, if Nigel forgave him at all.

When their plates were cleared away and replaced by an assortment of biscuits, cakes, and fruit, Penelope turned to her sister. Whatever she had been about to say died on her lips; she reached out and took Jane's hand.

"Dearest, you seem unwell," she said.

The imp's fingers closed convulsively over her sister's. "N-no. I am fine."

"Are you certain? You do look a trifle pale," Sebastian ventured.

A tenuous smile shaded her mouth. "Yes, thank you, my lord."

Pen did not seem convinced. "Perhaps you would like to take a brief turn down one of the walks and get some air," she suggested. "Lord Langley, would you be good enough to escort her?"

Lady Portia waved a dismissive hand. "No need to deprive us of his lordship's company, Penelope. And I fear Jane cannot appreciate Lord Nigel's sophistication as I do, so perhaps Mr. Havelock could spare a few moments for her."

Penelope shook her head. "Mr. Havelock has already offered to show me the ruins of the Gothic temple on the South Walk, Mama."

In response to this pronouncement, several things happened at once: Lady Portia began an outraged protest; Nigel piped up with "I'll go"; and Miss Jane grew quite pale.

Did no one else value the girl's company but her sister? She did not deserve to be treated with such indifference.

His jaw tense, Sebastian set aside his napkin and rose. "Perhaps we might all enjoy a brief promenade before the fireworks begin. Do not fret, Lady Portia—I would not consider depriving you of Nigel's company. And, as Miss Rutledge has a previous commitment, I happily render my services to your other daughter. Miss Jane, would you do me the honor?"

Jane flicked an uneasy glance at her sister, who made a little gesture of encouragement. Slowly, she climbed to her feet and accepted his hand. He led her down the Grand Cross Walk, away from her mother's shrill and strident voice. Paper lanterns lit the paths with a gentle glow; a cool evening breeze set them swaying.

"I should not have come," she said quietly.

"What, and miss all the excitement?" Sebastian drawled. "I was not certain what would explode first—the fireworks, or your mother."

She did not smile at this sally. She did not even look at him. "I did not wish to become an obligation to anyone."

"You are not an obligation," he assured her.

"I disagree, my lord. I know very well that my presence here is unwanted."

"Not by me."

Color flooded her face. "That is very gallant of you, but you should reserve your flattery for my sister."

"Do you not deserve to be flattered?"

She kept her gaze fixed on the path ahead of them. "Not by a gentleman who intends to marry someone else."

Sebastian inhaled sharply, as though someone had struck him in the ribs. Of course! He had been a fool not to recognize it earlier—the awkward silences, the lingering glances, the flush that stole into her cheeks when he teased her.

Jane Rutledge was in love with him.

He winced. This wasn't supposed to happen. He had done nothing to encourage her—or had he? He thought about that afternoon in the garden, about demanding a kiss from her. About riding with her in Hyde Park and sharing some of his most private thoughts. He shook himself. He'd bungled things. Nigel had been right.

He cleared his throat. "Tell me, Miss Jane," he began, "did you come to London to find a husband as well?"

"Just when I believe myself accustomed to your impertinence, my lord, you find a new way to surprise me," she replied with a hint of reproof.

"That is, what do you intend to do once your sister marries? Will you remain in Town?"

Her lips thinned. "I think not."

"May I ask why?"

"I have no reason to stay."

"None?" He lowered his head toward hers in a conspiratorial fashion. "Is there no gentleman who has captured your fancy?"

She closed her eyes briefly, then raised her chin at a defiant angle. "If there were, my lord, I should hardly confess it to you."

"You wound me, imp."

"Please stop calling me that."

"Why?"

"Because . . ." She appeared to gather her composure. "Because it makes me uncomfortable."

"Forgive me." He looked down at her hand on his arm, at her slender fingers encased in kidskin. It seemed ages ago that he had held that same hand, scratched and muddied, in his own. He exhaled in a slow sigh. "Will you be leaving very soon after the wedding?"

"As soon as possible. My mother may choose to remain for a few weeks—London has always held a particular . . . delight for her. But I have too much to do at home."

He chuckled. "What can you possibly have to do in Leicestershire that you cannot do here?"

"A great many things, my lord," she replied tightly.

"Such as?"

He should not bait her like this, but he found he could not help himself. He enjoyed their back and forth volleys and pointed, witty exchanges. Penelope, though engaging, was not half so clever as her younger sister.

"I must oversee matters at Wellbourne Grange," she answered.

"Surely that is a job better suited to your mother or to your steward."

"No. Wellbourne is my inheritance, and therefore my responsibility."

"Your inheritance? Your father left the stables to you?" he asked, unable to hide his surprise.

"Does that shock you?" she shot back, a challenge evident in her stormy eyes. "It certainly astonished everyone else. It was the talk of the county for months. Penelope received the lion's share of Papa's fortune, and I inherited Wellbourne. No one seems to think a woman competent to breed and train horses for the hunt." She made a moue. "It isn't ladylike."

"Somehow, I do not think that would stop you."

A look of unexpected gratitude lit her face, and she nodded. "It was the most practical solution. Papa had no son, and the estate was not entailed, so he wanted to make sure both Pen and I received an equal portion. I had helped him in the stables for years, and he trusted me to manage it well, so he left Wellbourne to me."

"I would never question your father's motives," he ventured, "but is that not a rather heavy burden to place on so young a lady?"

"No greater than what we have endured already," she murmured. "I shall manage."

Sebastian frowned, gripped by a protective desire he

could not explain. "Be reasonable, my dear—you cannot run the stable by yourself. You should find a husband who will do the worrying for you. If you stay in London, I know several gentlemen who would—"

She halted and yanked her arm from his grasp, her countenance pale with anger, her eyes bright and fierce. "So you would find me a husband, my lord?"

Passersby began to regard them with unseemly interest. Sebastian moved to take her arm again, but she backed out of his reach.

He held up his hands. "No need to fly up into the boughs. I am not funning you. I made the offer in earnest."

"Which makes it all the more insulting. Do you mean to imply that I am not capable of finding a husband, or that I am not attractive enough to snare one on my own?"

Sebastian tamped down a spurt of annoyance. "That is not what I meant."

Her hands tightened into fists; she held her arms rigidly at her sides. "Thank you for your generous offer of assistance," she said, biting off each word, "but I assure you it is completely unnecessary. I am already engaged."

Her words sunk in to his fevered mind. He scowled. "Engaged? To whom?"

"To a neighbor whose lands march with mine."

"And just when did this occur?"

She flushed. "Before we arrived in London."

"I see." He had a sudden vision of a country squire, well fed and bucolic, and the anger he kept restrained roared to life. She had played the innocent, sighing and casting forlorn glances in his direction, when all the while she was engaged to another man. Heat sizzled through his veins. "Why did you not tell me this from the start?"

"Would it have mattered?" she said bitterly. "You had eyes for no one but my sister."

"You little hypocrite," he snapped. "I remember a time when you would have let me kiss you, with your betrothed none the wiser."

She gasped; all traces of color fled her face.

His lips twisted in a sneer. "If you cared a whit for your honor and dignity, or that of your affianced, you would never have allowed yourself to fall in love with me."

He did not think it possible, but she turned paler still, her skin so ashen that he feared she might faint. "You are quite right, my lord," she replied, a catch in her voice. Her eyes glistened with unshed tears. "How could I have been so stupid?"

Lifting her skirts, she turned on her heel and fled.

A few women in the crowd of bystanders gasped; Sebastian realized that several members of the *ton* had just observed the entire scene. Word would be all over London by morning.

"Bloody hell," he muttered, and took off in pursuit.

It should not have mattered to him that the imp was betrothed, but dammit, it *did*. She had not lied to him, but neither had she told him the truth. He had not felt betrayal like this in years—over five years, to be exact—and he reacted now as he had then. She had hurt him, and he had lashed out at her for no other reason than to salve his wounded pride. And now both of them faced public humiliation.

There was still time to undo the damage. He needed to find her and apologize, then get her back to her mother and explain what had happened before any of the gossip made its way to Lady Portia. He fervently hoped that Penelope would still want to marry him when this was all over. For the moment, though, he had to find Jane. Vauxhall was no place for a woman alone.

She had run off toward the south along the Grand Cross Walk; Sebastian's eyes strained to catch a glimpse of a small figure in a white satin gown. There she was, passing the junction with the South Walk. He had to catch her before she went any farther; once she reached the Dark Walk, or the Lover's Walk as it was known, she was as good as ruined.

His longer stride closed the distance between them very quickly. Just before the intersection with the Dark Walk she looked over her shoulder and saw him; she tried to dart into the trees, but he caught her by the arm and brought her up short.

"Jane, wait," he gasped, breathing hard.

She tried to pull away. "Let go of me."

"Not until you listen to what I have to say."

"You have said quite enough," she snapped.

Even in the shadows of the trees that lined the walkway he could see the anger and hurt in her face. Her lips trembled, and her breasts rose and fell in rapid rhythm. During her wild flight a few locks of hair had come loose from their pins and tumbled into her eyes. He reached out and brushed them away; she flinched from his touch. He sighed.

"You cannot venture down these paths by yourself," he said. "It's too dangerous."

"So I see," she replied a trifle petulantly.

She tugged again at her arm, but he did not loosen his grasp.

The warmth of her body seeped through his gloves. The cool evening breeze ruffled his hair and brought with it the faint scent of lilac; he remembered holding her shawl, inhaling that same perfume. She smelled of the outdoors, of lilacs and warm skin. He leaned closer and brushed his lips over her hair. A faint moan escaped her.

"What are you doing?" she whispered.

"I am trying to apologize," he murmured in reply.

"This . . . is a most singular apology, my lord."

"Sebastian."

She ducked her head.

He tucked a finger beneath her chin and raised it again. Her huge eyes searched his face.

"I want to hear you say my name," he said.

The tip of her tongue skimmed her lower lip. His mouth went dry.

"Say it," he cajoled.

"Why are you doing this to me, Sebastian?" she breathed.

A thrill shot through him. The way she said his name, in the barest whisper of sound, tantalized him more than the erotic utterances of any mistress he had ever known.

He ignored her question and focused instead on the lush curves of her mouth. He snaked one arm around her waist, his hand resting at the small of her back, then pulled her to him. She did not resist.

"You are such a fey creature," he murmured. He tucked a strand of hair behind her ear, then traced its soft, curved outline with the tip of one finger.

She shivered. "Let me go. Please, Sebastian."

His fingers trailed down the line of her neck, over the soft indentation at the hollow of her throat where her pulse throbbed in an erratic rhythm.

"Not until I collect that kiss," he heard himself say.

His mouth feathered over hers, teasing, testing, before he claimed it entirely. She moaned and tipped her head back, her body bent like a young willow. His tongue slipped past her parted lips. She tasted of wine and strawberries; he drank her in as a man would water in the desert until every nerve in his body thrummed with awareness.

She whimpered, a tiny sound deep in her throat, and Sebastian raised his lips from hers. Egad. He would never have guessed that so much desire lurked beneath that solemn exterior! She had come alive in his arms, her breasts pressed against him, her hands gripping his lapels for dear life. She had even kissed him back, for God's sake!

Her kiss, though inexperienced, made his blood burn for more. His contrary little imp possessed more passion in her little finger than her sister could ever hope to have.

Her sister.

His heart stopped mid-beat.

God in heaven, what had he done?

"I say, Langley, which Rutledge girl are you after?" cawed a raucous voice. "Or do you intend to sample the charms of each one before you make your decision?"

She stiffened; Sebastian tightened his arms around her. In a loose cluster on the walkway stood a group of fashionably dressed bucks, watching and chortling among themselves. The viscount recognized a few faces; these fellows must have seen the argument, then followed after him and Jane in the hopes of seeing more. And they had, indeed.

"Bundle yourselves off, you pack of jackanapes, or face me in Hyde Park at dawn tomorrow," he snarled.

The young men laughed; some jeered. A few made mocking bows before sauntering on their way.

Sebastian looked down at the woman he held in his arms. She rested her forehead against his chest and hunched into his embrace.

"You realize what this means, don't you?" he asked quietly.

She drew a long, shuddering breath. "Yes. It means we are utterly ruined."

Chapter Six

"How could you do this to me?" Lady Portia shrilled. "You selfish, ungrateful girl—I vow you did this on purpose, to disgrace me. I shall never be able to show my face in public again!"

Jane stood in the middle of the drawing room floor, her spine straight and her head held high, blinking furiously at the tears that pooled on her lashes. She would not cry. She must not. If she showed any weakness, her mother would make mincemeat of her. Not that the situation could get any worse; her dignity was in shreds, and she felt a deep, overwhelming sense of shame.

She had predicted that Lady Portia would fly up into the boughs when she and Sebastian—Lord Langley— returned and explained what had happened. But she had not expected the cold, cruel, deliberate rage that gripped her mother. The fact that they had not been able to locate Penelope and Mr. Havelock right away only served to fuel her fury. Though Lord Nigel had gallantly volunteered to stay behind and look for them, it had not placated Lady Portia one whit.

Viscount Langley had taken Jane and her mother home, then retired to his house next door, with the promise that he would call on them the next afternoon. Jane supposed she should be happy; Sebastian was going to offer her the protection of his name. Not that either of them had any choice after this evening's debacle.

Why on earth had she let him kiss her? He had teased, patronized, and humiliated her, then pursued and waylaid her when she had made it clear that she wanted nothing more to do with him. Or had she? She should have protested with greater vehemence. She should have run straight back to the supper box. She should have—

No. What was done was done, no matter how much she might regret it. She must stand and face the consequences, not the least of which was her mother's furious tirade. But nothing Lady Portia said could make Jane feel any more miserable than she did already. She had stolen Penelope's beau, a man she loved. She had betrayed her own sister in the worst possible way.

"Are you listening to me, Jane?" demanded her mother.

Jane jumped. Her heart leaped into her throat.

Lady Portia crossed the Aubusson carpet with deliberate steps, her blue eyes glittering, her expression livid. "You have always been a selfish, jealous, thoughtless creature. Penelope did nothing to merit this hateful deed."

"I have never been jealous of my sister," Jane replied tightly.

Her mother stiffened. "Of course you have. You resent her because she is beautiful and has greater prospects than you could ever hope to have. I will see to it that she makes a brilliant match, which is certain now that you will no longer be here to poison her against me."

"I would never do anything so vile," she insisted.

"Do not lie to me, you little vixen. I know what is best

for Penelope, yet you have subverted my authority at every turn."

"I have done no such thing!"

"Have you not?" Lady Portia reached into her reticule and pulled out a small, familiar, leather-bound journal.

A yawning pit seemed to open up beneath Jane's feet. Her mother had found the List.

Lady Portia waved the book in her face. "This is your fault. Penelope knows her duty to me. She would never have considered doing something like this if not for your malicious influence."

"Pen is not a doll, Mama, for you to dress up and manipulate at your whim," she replied through clenched teeth. Anger blazed through her; her head felt as though it no longer rested on her shoulders. "Whether you like it or not, she has a mind of her own, and she will not allow you to bully her into marriage as compensation for your own disappointments."

"How dare you speak to me that way!" her mother snapped. "I have made countless sacrifices on your behalf, and *this* is how you repay me? You should be thankful I gave birth to you at all."

Jane's eyes narrowed. "What do you mean?"

"I never wanted you," Lady Portia declared with a cold, superior air. "Penelope is perfect in every way; I wanted no more children after she was born. You have been nothing but a burden, you with your plain face and willful ways."

She blinked away an angry barrage of tears. "Papa never thought so."

Lady Portia sniffed in disdain. "Your father was a countrified fool, just as you are. Do you really think you will be able to retain the interest of a Corinthian like Viscount Langley? In no time at all he will grow weary of seeing your mousy countenance every morning at the breakfast table and take up with a string of mistresses. And I, for one, would not blame him."

The angry retort slipped out before Jane could stop it: "Is that what you did to Papa, once you grew tired of him and the farm? You did not make all those trips to London just to visit your ailing cousin."

Lady Portia landed a stinging slap on Jane's cheek.

Jane took the blow in silence, though her ears rang with the force of it. "Papa knew," she said, her voice rough. "He knew everything. Why else do you suppose your widow's portion is so small?"

Her mother paled, her lips compressed into a bloodless line. "I have nothing more to say to you. Go to your room, Jane, and stay there until I call for you. I shall remain here and wait for Penelope. I should never have allowed her to go off with that ill-bred tradesman."

Jane departed from the overheated drawing room, her back ramrod straight, then marched up the stairs. A sigh of relief escaped her when she escaped her mother's oppressive presence.

She raised a trembling hand to her still tingling cheek. Her mother's words had flayed her to the quick — with one exception. Her mother seemed convinced that Lord Langley would be a worse husband to her than he would to Penelope, simply because Jane was not beautiful. Did she really believe that physical attractiveness had any effect on a husband's loyalty and respect for his wife? From what Jane had seen, a man's character did not fluctuate according to the beauty of the woman he married. One had but to observe the way he treated others to know what sort of person he was. And, for the most part, Viscount Langley seemed to be an honorable gentleman.

He had not meant to compromise her. It had just—happened. . . .

No. That was not true. She was no more the victim than he. They had both allowed matters to progress this far. And she could not for the life of her imagine why.

No, that was not true, either. She knew why she had done it—she loved him. Despite her best intentions, her agreement with Augustus, and her devotion to Pen, she had fallen in love with Viscount Langley. His charm, his amiable nature, and his irrepressible roguish grin had proved too much for her to resist.

She loved him, and he knew it. He had seen through all her attempts at pretense. But he must feel something for her in return; his kiss had seared her soul. Even now she could feel the warmth of his hands on her body, the taste of his mouth and tongue. She shivered. What would it be like to be married to such a passionate man?

She shivered again, this time from apprehension. Augustus. What would she tell him? He deserved to hear about this from her, not from a society gossip column in London newspapers. She would have to write to him tomorrow and explain matters in person when they returned to Leicestershire. Her hasty marriage would put a strain on their neighborly relations, but that could not be helped.

When Jane reached her bedchamber, she thought about ringing for McBride, but decided against it; her mother's dresser would be no less censorious than Lady Portia herself. She took off the white satin gown, her fingers lingering on the tiny rosebuds along the neckline. Tears spilled over her lashes, and she made no move to stop them. Oh, God, what was she going to tell Pen? She loved her sister above all else in the world; she could not bear to lose her. Would she believe their mother's story, that Jane had done this on purpose? No, Pen knew her too well to credit such gammon. Jane would simply have to tell her the complete truth, as painful as it would be for both of them, and hope that her sister forgave her.

She laid the dress gently over the back of a chair; she would return it to Pen in the morning—that is, if her sister was still speaking to her. She brushed out her hair, changed into her night rail, then climbed into bed.

Apprehension made her restless, and both her body and her mind refused to relax enough to sleep. She sat up and rearranged the pillows on her bed. Perhaps reading would help.

She reached into the drawer of her bedside table and retrieved her book. Strange . . . there seemed to be something inside it.

What in the world . . . ?

Jane pulled forth a small, unmarked envelope. Where had this come from? She opened it, frowning. Inside was a letter, written in her sister's neat and elegant hand.

Dearest,
I must apologize for this deception. I had to leave this note where no one but you would find it; I could not take the chance that McBride might discover it and warn anyone—especially Mama—of my plans.

Questions crowded Jane's mind. Her plans? What was she talking about? When had she put this letter in Jane's book? And where in heaven's name was she? She pursed her lips and read on:

Mama has the List. I discovered it missing from its hiding place this afternoon, and I knew I had to act quickly. You told me that I would know when to set

*the List aside and follow my heart. My dearest Jane,
I am doing just that—by the time you read this I will
be on my way to Gretna Green with Jason Havelock.*

Gretna Green? Penelope had eloped!

Jane set the letter in her lap and stared blindly into
space. Who would have thought . . . Sweet, shy Penelope
would never . . . She couldn't . . . *Elope?* And with Mr.
Havelock? She forced herself to read that portion of the
letter again; no, she had not misread it. And there was
more . . .

*I did not intend to fall in love with him. I had
resigned myself to accepting the attentions of Lord
Langley, but the more I saw of Jace, the more I came
to know him, the more I realized I could not marry
the viscount. Then Jace kissed me at the
Peterboroughs' ball and asked me to elope with him.
To be his wife. And I knew then that was what I
wanted more than anything else in the world!*

Jane remembered her sister's swollen lips and dazed
expression the night of the ball and her troubled demeanor afterward, and everything fit together. Oh, if only
Pen had told her!

*Jace respects my opinions, dearest—respects me,
and does not treat me as a flighty, featherheaded
miss whose value as a person is measured by either
her beauty or her dowry. He is everything I desire—
handsome, kind, generous, thoughtful, well-spoken—
and he loves me. He loves me as I love him. I do not
care that he has no title. Our mother will never
understand, but I know you will.*

I wanted to confide in you, dearest, desperately so, but I could not take the chance that McBride might overhear even the merest mention of my affection for Jason Havelock, much less our plans. I can only pray that you will forgive me.

"Of course I do," Jane murmured. An ache began deep in her chest.

I regret that I have left you to deal with Mama. I would not have resorted to such scandalous methods if I had thought she would approve Jace's suit, but both you and I know how she feels on that score. I had no other choice, dearest—if I stayed, Mama would have forced me to marry Viscount Langley, and I could not wed a man I do not love.

I shall not see you again for some time. Once Jace and I are married, we will board his ship, the Paladin, *and set sail for the West Indies. It is our hope that, by the time we return, the scandal will have subsided, and that our friends and family will have recovered from the shock and be able to pardon us.*

I shall miss you, Jane. I promise to write as often as possible and will count the days until I see you again.

> *Your loving and devoted sister,*
> *Penelope*

A tear trickled down Jane's cheek before she realized she was crying. Pen . . . in love. With a man she found worthy—who *was* worthy, even though he had no title. And she had defied her mother to be with him. Pen, who had rarely stood up for herself, had found courage in her love for Mr. Havelock. Jane wanted to cheer, but the sound that emerged from her throat was half-laugh, half-sob.

Dear, dear Pen. Oh, how she would miss her! Jane hiccuped, then forced herself to draw a deep, even breath. Her gaze alighted on her sister's dress, and realization struck her. Lady Portia would not want anything more to do with her after this scandal. With Pen gone, she was alone. The loss struck her like a physical blow. Even after the death of their father, Penelope had always stood by her, her loving support true and unwavering. Now she had no one.

No, that was not true. She had Lord Langley. But would a worldly gentleman such as he be interested in a place like Wellbourne?

Jane hugged her knees to her chest. She could rely upon him, couldn't she? For all his condescending manner, he had seemed genuinely concerned about her managing the farm by herself. Once they married, Wellbourne Grange would become his by law. Surely he would not take the farm and its assets to do with as he pleased. He was heir to a great earldom; he had no need for her estate or the income it produced.

She shook herself. It did her no good to fret. Pen was gone, and Jane had no choice but to marry the viscount. So many changes to her life, and all in one evening! She would worry about the stables later, once she and Sebastian had time to talk.

For the moment, though, she had business to attend to. Jane donned her dressing gown and, Pen's letter in hand, headed back downstairs.

A mischievous smile crooked her mouth. Perhaps she

should warn McBride to have her mother's smelling salts ready; Lady Portia was in for another nasty surprise.

By the next morning the Rutledge sisters were the talk of London. After considering the suit of some of England's most eligible bachelors, Miss Penelope Rutledge, heiress and reigning Toast of the Season, had run off to Gretna Green with a shipowner, the son of a Devonshire squire. And Miss Jane Rutledge had shared a very passionate, very public embrace near the Dark Walk in Vauxhall Gardens with her sister's most prominent admirer. That afternoon so many gossipmongers called on Jane's mother under the pretense of expressing their sympathies that eventually Lady Portia ordered the butler to inform visitors that she was not at home to anyone except Lord Langley, who dutifully presented himself at their front door at half past three and was admitted posthaste.

Jane thought the viscount took the news of Pen's elopement surprisingly well; only the twitch of a muscle at his temple and the tight set of his jaw betrayed any anger. Caught between his intent, unsmiling demeanor and Lady Portia's glacial glare, Jane was quite willing to make herself scarce when the viscount asked to speak with her mother in private.

When Lady Portia emerged at last from the drawing room, she ignored Jane completely, sweeping past her and up the stairs. Lord Langley—Sebastian—appeared in the doorway and motioned for her to join him.

"What did you say to her?" Jane asked, after he closed the door behind them.

"Nothing that did not need to be said," he replied, and shrugged. "I fear your mother holds neither of us in very great esteem."

She smiled faintly. "You have a talent for understatement, my lord."

"From what I understand, she wanted your sister to marry a peer but was content to see you wedded to a country squire. And now the opposite has happened. We have managed to turn the entire world upside down."

Jane crossed the carpet to stand before the fireplace, rubbing her hands over her arms to dispel a sudden chill. The viscount regarded her with none of the warmth or kindness he had shown last night. What had her mother told him? But wait—he had cultivated this aloof manner from the moment he entered the house. A knot of dread coiled in her stomach. Was he having second thoughts?

No, she was being ridiculous. He was an honorable man; there had to be another explanation. Perhaps weariness rode him as hard as it did her. He looked as though he had not slept at all. Dark circles smudged the skin under his flinty eyes, and lines of weariness pulled at his mouth.

He ambled toward the bow window, his hands clasped behind his back. "I will have the special license by tomorrow morning, and we can be wed any time after that," he announced, "although, given the gossip being bruited about, I would counsel more than a modicum of haste."

Another shiver shot down Jane's spine. "As you wish, my lord."

He turned. "Good. Then let's get this over with. Miss Jane, would you do me the honor of becoming my wife?"

Jane stood as though rooted to the floor. Her gaze searched his face, but his fierce expression did not alter. This was a formality, true, but she could detect little affection in his manner, and none of his incorrigible charm. He seemed almost . . . resentful.

"Well?" he asked, impatient.

"Yes, my lord. I will marry you," she answered in a strangled voice.

He sighed, and the hard lines of his face seemed to soften. He rubbed the bridge of his nose. "I'm sorry, imp," he said. "Neither of us imagined things would turn out this way. Will a day be enough for you to get ready?"

She wrapped her arms around her body. "It should."

He nodded. "Then I will make the arrangements with your mother. But I regret I cannot stay. If you will excuse me, I will leave you to your preparations."

"Of course," she replied woodenly.

He made her a brief bow, then departed.

Jane stared after him, stunned. In no way did the man who had just asked her to marry him resemble the man who had kissed her so passionately last night. Which was the real Sebastian, and which one had she just agreed to wed?

The question plagued her well into the evening. Lady Portia took dinner in her rooms, which suited Jane very well. She had never gotten along with her mother, but now the relationship between them had degenerated to outright hostility. Lady Portia had spent most of the day draped over a chaise in the drawing room, moaning about how she was ruined and how her life would never be the same. Jane uttered a distinctly unladylike snort. Never mind showing any concern for either of her daughters; Lady Portia's first thoughts were always for herself.

The evening was warm, so Jane sat at her open bedroom window, enjoying the breeze and the silence of the house. She could still hear noises from the direction of the street, but here above the garden they were faint enough for her to ignore.

Such a strange day. She retrieved her hairbrush and began brushing out her hair in long, even strokes. The simple act soothed her, calming nerves worn ragged from distress. She leaned back in her chair, her eyes half closed.

The sound of raised voices roused her. She sat up and looked out the window.

"Dammit, Nigel, it wasn't supposed to happen this way!"

Her throat closed in a convulsive swallow. That was Sebastian's voice. The scent of cheroot smoke drifted past her nose. He must be in his garden. She set down her brush and began to close the window—she did not wish to eavesdrop again. Lord Nigel's reply, however, froze her where she stood.

"Yet it did, old fellow, and you're stuck. Does the chit have any money at all?"

"Not *per se*—she has a large property in south Leicestershire. A stud farm. Can you image me as a stable boy, Nigel?" Disgust tainted the viscount's words. "Damn Jace! He knew I needed Miss Rutledge's fortune, yet made off with her anyway. Friend or no, I should like nothing better than to thrash him."

Jane removed her shaking hands from the window sash.

"I fear the signs were right under our very noses," Nigel said mournfully. "The way he looked at her, the way he always managed to insert himself next to her in any crowd. He cast sheep's eyes at her for days."

"He confronted me after I kissed Miss Rutledge at the Peterboroughs' ball," the viscount added with a growl. "Dammit, I knew he'd formed a *tendre* for her, but I never thought he would act on it."

"Perhaps we both underestimated him." Lord Nigel paused. "You know he would not have done something like this on a whim."

"Are you defending him?"

Another pause. "I am merely saying that he would never have deliberately hurt you. Did his note give any explanation at all?"

"He said he loved Penelope too much to see me ruin her." Sebastian snorted. "I had no intention of doing anything to her."

"Except helping yourself to her lovely fortune," Nigel drawled. "And it did not hurt that she was one of the most beautiful creatures in London."

"Of course."

"Then what do you plan to do with the mousy little antidote?" Nigel asked.

Antidote? Jane's fingers curled inward so tightly that her fingernails bit into her palms.

"I am not certain," the viscount confessed. "But I do know I have to marry her. If I cry off now, I will not only earn my father's wrath, but that of every other female in Town. No heiress would have me then, and I would be even worse off."

"You could still accept the quarterly allowance from your father."

"Like hell I could. I need to have an independent source of funds, Nigel. I refuse to let that old bastard use his money to manipulate me."

"Here is an idea. If the chit's stables produce halfway decent bits of blood, you should be able to fetch a good price for them at Tatt's. Or what about selling off some of the land? Either way, you could pay off your debts and be able to return to your life as a knight of the green baize with plenty of the ready."

"I had not thought of that."

A buzzing began in Jane's ears. She sank back down into her seat, her vision beginning to blur at the edges.

The rumors about Sebas—Viscount Langley—were true. He was a gangster. A wastrel.

A liar.

She gripped the arms of her chair. His every action had been steeped in deception. His courtship of Penelope. Their friendship.

Their kiss.

Only now did she realize that he felt nothing for her, with the possible exception of contempt. And it sounded like he fully intended to plunder her stables to fund his profligate lifestyle. Nausea swelled within her.

She could not marry him. No—she must. Though she had visions of jilting him at the altar, such notions were pure fancy. After what had happened last night, she could not go back to Leicestershire unwed. She could not besmirch her father's memory or his name.

Besides, no one would buy prime cattle from a woman of notorious reputation. Well . . . some gentlemen might, and try to bargain for other services in the process. She shuddered at the thought. Augustus would not marry her; she had already sent the letter to him. Even if she had not, Augustus Wingate was enough of a high stickler that, after hearing the gossip from London, he would not want anything further to do with her. She had to marry Lord Langley.

No—wait! There was one more thing she could do. Her mouth tightened.

She crossed the room to her escritoire, took out a blank piece of parchment, and began to write another letter.

Sebastian and Lady Portia had arranged a quiet marriage ceremony. The clergyman would perform the service in the drawing room of the Rutledge's town house, with Lady Portia and Lord Nigel serving as witnesses. No pomp, no celebration—none of the traditional trappings associated with a Society wedding. All parties involved wanted this done as quickly and quietly as possible, Sebastian most of all.

Blast. In a few moments he would be a married man, but with little to show for it save a wife and some ramshackle collection of fields and barns in Leicestershire. He should never have allowed the situation at Vauxhall to get out of hand, But he had, and now he would pay the price for it. The hunter found himself caged.

Everything about the situation rankled him; it did not help that the imp had gazed at him with her heart in her eyes. He did not want her love. Love was poor currency; it could not purchase what he truly wanted.

A foul temper gripped him when he and Nigel arrived at the Rutledge residence a few minutes before the appointed hour. The dour-faced butler took their hats and gloves and motioned them into the drawing room.

"Lord Langley, may I speak with you a moment?"

Sebastian raised his head toward the source of the voice; Jane stood at the top of the stairs, dressed in the rose pink gown she had worn to the Symingtons' ball. She wore her dark hair up, with a few wispy strands left loose to frame her impossibly high cheekbones. On the whole, she appeared very soft and vulnerable—until he looked into her eyes.

Her gray gaze held all the warmth of polished steel.

"Will you excuse us, Lord Nigel?" Steel laced her voice as well.

Nigel arched a blond brow at him. He nodded. His friend sketched a brief bow to Jane, then disappeared into the drawing room.

"What is this about, Jane?" he asked, tamping down

his irritation. "Can this not wait until after the ceremony?"

"We have time; the minister has yet to arrive. Let us go into the garden, my lord."

She started toward the back of the house. He followed her, noting the rigid set of her shoulders. She wasn't going to cry off, was she? Damnation. If she did, they would both be in the suds. Now was not the time for a fit of maidenly vapors.

When they reached the garden, Jane gestured toward a stone bench beneath the familiar knobby elm. "Do sit down."

"I prefer to stand, thank you," he replied brusquely.

She shrugged. "As you wish. I have no desire to delay the ceremony, my lord, so I will come right to 'the point. I overheard your discussion with Lord Nigel yesterday evening. My window, you see, overlooks the garden. It's the one up there, on the left. You really must learn to temper your vehemence, my lord; this is not the first time I have heard something I should not have."

Sebastian's head jerked toward the garden wall. Damn! He had forgotten how well sound carried over the brick partition. His anger and frustration had made him careless. Well, he was trapped with the plaguey imp now, and there was no going back.

"I see. Then to which point of the conversation did you object?" he asked mockingly.

A hollow, ringing laugh burst from her throat. "To which point did I *not*?"

His jaw flexed. "And now you think you know everything."

She spared him a look of pure, unadulterated loathing. "I learned more about you last night than I ever did in the past two weeks. You are in debt from gambling, yet your pride will not allow you to accept money from your father. So you set your sights on an heiress—namely, my sister, as she was the most attractive one to be found. Why wed an antidote when you could have a beauty *and* her twenty-five thousand pounds? Once you were safely married, you would use her dowry as you pleased, then go back to your life of dissipation. You would not care one whit if you broke my sister's heart."

"Well, that point is rather moot, since your sister ran off with one of my best friends. A former best friend, I should say."

"Do you deny that was your plan?" she demanded, pinning him with a furious stare.

"No. And something tells me you would not believe me if I tried."

"I have every reason to mistrust you. You used me to get into my sister's good graces. You used your charm and the pretense of friendship to further your own ambition. And now that she has slipped through your fingers, you have set your sights on me.

"I suppose I should be flattered that you believe marriage to me is preferable to disinheritance. But I will not allow you to march into Wellbourne and start selling off my horses and my land to settle *your* debts. That farm is all I have left of my father, and I will not let you ruin it."

Sebastian struggled to contain his rising fury. The chit dared moralize to him after the way she had deceived her now-former betrothed?

"You mean sell *my* horses and *my* land," he snapped. "Wellbourne Grange will become mine when we marry."

"I am well aware of that."

"Then you are also aware that you will have little say in the matter." His temples began to throb with an insistent, painful rhythm. Hellfire and damnation, this was the last thing he wanted to deal with right now!

"So you will rank the demands of your pocketbook above those of our marriage?"

"You will be a viscountess, not the wife of some loutish squire, and that must be deemed an advantage.{

"To you, perhaps—not to me," she shot back. She paced a few steps away from him, turned, and paced back. "What a masterful stroke of irony! I wanted you when I could not have you, and now that I have you, I no longer want you."

"A bit late for that," he sneered. "In a few moments we will be husband and wife."

Tears glimmered in her eyes; she blinked them away. "I want you to know something before we complete that arrangement."

He folded his arms over his chest. "And what would that be?"

"I have written a letter to your father informing him of our marriage and the circumstances surrounding it, including your quest for an heiress."

"You *what*?"

"I told your father everything that had transpired between us. My family knows; so should yours."

A red haze misted his vision. "My God—what have you done?"

"The only thing I could, my lord, to ensure the safety of my inheritance. To that end, I propose a bargain. Since you have no interest in helping me manage the estate, I shall return to Leicestershire—alone. I shall pay your debts, and the stables will sustain your fashionable style of living. But if you gamble away so much as an acre of Wellbourne land or auction any of the horses, I will sell what remains of the estate to your father and disappear to the continent. Then you shall not have me, my land, or any notable source of income, nor shall you have the freedom to marry another heiress."

Sebastian gaped at her. Never had he seen the girl so fierce, so determined. If she had been solemn before, now she was absolutely grim. Her eyes held no trace of sparkle or vitality. *He* had done this to her. His wounded pride had goaded him to say some terrible things last night, none of which he had intended her to hear. But she had heard, and he could not take any of it back. The resentment and anger he had nursed since last night began to dissipate beneath in an overwhelming cloud of guilt.

"You forget one thing: I shall require an heir. Do you not want children?" he asked quietly.

"Even if I did, I could not imagine bringing them up in such appalling circumstances. I cannot imagine anything more horrid than growing up in a world where one's parents despise each other."

"But you do want them?"

She bit her lip; fresh tears shimmered on her lashes. "Yes."

"Then where does that leave us?"

"If—you honor your side of the agreement, then perhaps, in a year or so, we might . . ."

He took a step closer to her. "You are my wife. You cannot keep me from your bed forever."

"Would you force me?"

She sounded so vulnerable. And with those tears in her huge eyes, all he wanted to do was pull her into his arms and hold her as he had last night. He swallowed hard. "No."

"Then do you agree?" Her voice quavered.

His shoulders slumped. "Yes."

"Very well. Then let us go inside and have done with

it. We should not keep the minister waiting." Lifting her skirts, she strode past him and into the house.

Sebastian watched her go but did not follow immediately. He stood in the garden, more alone than he had ever been in his life.

He should be happy. Jane was giving him what he wanted most—his freedom. So why did he feel so utterly miserable?

Chapter Seven

Odd. He did not feel like a married man. That must be because he had no idea what the devil a married man was supposed to feel like. If it meant feeling drunk, unbearably empty, and sorry for oneself, then he supposed he'd gotten it right.

Nearly a month had passed since that ill-fated morning when he had exchanged vows with Jane Rutledge. His wife. Strange to think of her in such an intimate way. During the ceremony he had stood next to her, so near as to feel the warmth from her slender body, but never actually touched her until the end, when he had placed his ring on her finger and given her a chaste, gentle kiss. No sooner had his lips brushed hers than she pulled away, her face shuttered and pale. The memory of that contact, however brief, lingered with him.

The anger and resentment lingered as well. He had spent his wedding night alone and drunk as an emperor. Why not? He had gotten himself married and had nothing to show for it but injured pride and an empty bed.

His plan had been proceeding perfectly until *she* came along. He shouldn't even have been attracted to her; she was outspoken, forthright, and plain. Yet he was. And he had thrown all his carefully-laid schemes out the window for one kiss.

Now she had him on a leash. She had been as good as her word and paid his debts, but it rankled that he should be obligated to his wife for his living. Her property was his by law; legally he had complete ownership and control of Wellbourne Grange and could dispose of it as he pleased. But he could not bring himself to do it.

What the devil was the matter with him?

Determined to forget about his wife and his travesty of a marriage, Sebastian had returned to his former way of life, with Nigel's enthusiastic endorsement. He had patronized the lowest gaming hells, imbibed bottle after bottle of claret without fear of reproach, ogled opera dancers, and raced his chestnut mare through Hyde Park against all comers. Let the gossip get back to his wife in Leicestershire. That would show her he had no intention of mending his roguish ways.

But Fate, ever a fickle mistress, had other plans. Instead of losing at the gaming tables, he won, even when he wagered recklessly or on a whim. Just last night he had won over two thousand pounds from Sir Reginald Kettering. He found none of the opera dancers attractive; their overripe figures and painted faces revolted him. And two weeks ago his mare had pulled up lame, depriving him of another favorite pastime.

So here he sat, bored, half-foxed, and thoroughly out of temper. He hefted the bottle of wine, peered at the level of liquid within it, then set it aside. God's blood, he did not even have the desire to get himself properly foxed. Furious with himself, he vaulted out of his chair and headed for White's; at this hour of the day, he could usually find Nigel at the faro table.

Unfortunately Lord Nigel Barrington had never been

known for his constancy, and could be found neither at White's nor at Watier's. In fact, Sebastian had not seen the garrulous fellow for the past two days, and that troubled him. He had many acquaintances, but few friends. Jace was gone, and now Nigel had taken himself off without so much as a word.

Suddenly he felt unbearably lonely.

With a low growl, Sebastian returned home to dress for the evening. There had to be *something* in London with which he could distract himself.

He was halfway up the stairs when his butler stopped him.

"Ah . . . forgive me, my lord," the servant began.

"Yes, what is it, Cobb?" Sebastian asked with no little annoyance.

The portly man looked as though he had swallowed something that disagreed with him.

"Well?" demanded the viscount.

"Er . . . the Earl of Stanhope is waiting in the drawing room, my lord."

Sebastian's hand tightened on the iron stair railing. His father? Here?

"He insisted upon waiting, my lord," Cobb added.

"Yes, I am certain he did," muttered the viscount. After a moment's hesitation, he reversed direction and headed back down the staircase.

The Earl of Stanhope stood in front of the bow window, leaning heavily on his mahogany cane. Sebastian paused in the drawing room doorway and studied his father's profile. Though the man's shoulders seemed increasingly bent with age, the rest of his appearance remained unchanged. Faded hair that was once a deep brown waved away from his forehead. Hawk-like blue eyes presided above a straight aristocratic nose and a strong jaw. The resemblance was unmistakable; Sebastian would probably look like this when he got on in years. A strong sense of loathing gripped him.

"Good afternoon, my lord," he said, his lips curled in disdain. "To what do I owe the dubious pleasure of this visit?"

The earl turned; his sharp blue gaze settled on Sebastian.

"Ah, there you are," Lord Stanhope replied. "I was beginning to think you would never return."

"If I had known you were here, I would not have," the viscount assured him.

A dry chuckle rattled in his father's throat. "Still angry with me, I see."

"Why should I not be?" Sebastian snarled, then checked himself. "What do you want?"

"Will you not invite me to sit down?"

His face wooden, Sebastian gestured to one of the claw-footed chairs near the fireplace.

Lord Stanhope sat down slowly, supporting himself on his cane. His left leg did not bend, but stuck out at a stiff angle.

Sebastian remained standing. "I take it this is not a social call."

"No, indeed."

"I have fulfilled your stipulations, my lord. We can have little more to say to each other."

"On the contrary," replied the earl. "We have a great deal to discuss, beginning with your wife."

A tremor of foreboding quivered at the base of Sebastian's spine. "I have been married over a month, my lord. 'Tis a bit late to express displeasure with my choice."

"Actually, she intrigues me. Plucky sort of girl. If you happen to like pluck."

The viscount glared at him. "What do *you* know of her?"

"Very little, really, other than what I was able to glean from her letter."

Sebastian ground his teeth. Her letter. Of course.

"I did a bit of checking into her family," Lord Stanhope continued. "Her father left her some property in Leicestershire, I believe."

"Yes," he intoned. What was the old despot getting at?

"I am merely curious to learn why she is there, and you are here and have been since your wedding."

The viscount grimaced. It all made sense. Now that he was married, the next topic of discussion would be grandchildren and how soon he could produce them. "That, my lord, is none of your business."

Lord Stanhope rested both his hands atop his cane and sighed. "You have never liked me, have you, boy?"

"Like you?" Sebastian almost laughed. "Oh, come now, sir, let us be frank. I loathe you."

"Why?"

The question took the viscount by surprise. "I should think it obvious."

"Then humor me."

"All right, then. Where to begin? As far back as I can remember, you pitted Alex and me against each other. You held him up as a paragon of virtue, but you never had a kind word for me. In fact, the only time you ever spoke to me was to criticize me for some real or imagined wrong."

The earl nodded. "Go on."

"I might have forgiven you if not for one thing."

"And what might that be?"

Sebastian stared up at his brother's portrait about the

mantelpiece, his heart constricted in a painful knot. "You killed Alex."

The earl glanced at the portrait and flinched.

"Do you deny it?" Sebastian demanded.

The old man's shoulders slumped, and he shook his head. "No."

Sebastian stared. "What did you say?"

"I never gave you a detailed account of what happened, did I?"

"You never bothered to mention it at all."

Lord Stanhope seemed to hunch into himself; the lines in his face deepened. "I had thought to spare you, but I see now I erred too much on the side of caution. At Christmastide five years ago I suffered an attack of apoplexy that left me almost completely paralyzed. My physician thought I would not live much longer, so I sent for your brother." He shook his head sadly. "Alexander was determined to reach me, blizzard be damned."

Sebastian slid into the nearest chair, stunned. "Apoplexy?"

The earl gestured to his leg. "Did you never wonder how I came by this?"

"Why did you not tell me?"

"I did not think you would care to know."

"Then Alex . . . You did not order him . . ."

"I blame myself for what happened," the earl said in a heavy voice. "I sent for him because I was a selfish, fretful old man—I did not wish to die alone."

Emotion clogged the back of Sebastian's throat, and he fought to suppress a sudden onslaught of tears. He swallowed hard. He'd be damned if he displayed such frailty in front of his father.

"All this time I blamed you for separating us," he said harshly. "Alex and I had just started to become friends for the first time in our lives. Then you summoned him home and ripped him away from me just as I was getting to know him. I hated you for that. I thought you had done it on purpose."

The earl's gaze softened. "I know."

"You knew? What do you mean, you knew?" Sebastian gripped the arms of his chair. "You let me revile you as a tyrant, yet you said nothing. I blamed you for Alex's death—still you said nothing. You ignored me for the better part of five years. Why?"

"It took me that long to recover the use of my legs. I did not wish you to see me as a cripple."

Sebastian stared uncomprehendingly at his father. "But—Alex's funeral . . . You were not there . . ."

"I had paid my respects earlier from my Bath chair. In my pride, I did not wish to display the extent of my infirmity to all and sundry—including you."

"Why did you not tell me?"

"You might have thought to ask, rather than simply assume the worst," the earl rejoined. "And you did not have to inquire of me directly; any of the servants or staff would have revealed the truth."

The two of them stared at each other like duelists, until at last Sebastian dropped his gaze. He balled his hand into a fist and thumped it against the arm of his chair. All these years spent hating his father . . . over a misunderstanding. Between his stubbornness and his father's pride, the world had never seen a greater pair of fools. He lifted his head, his eyes narrowed at the earl. If he had been mistaken about his father's role in Alexander's death, what else had he misconstrued?

"So why are you telling me this now?"

Lord Stanhope shifted in his chair. "We are overdue for a talk, boy."

"Indeed? We have barely spoken two civil words to each other our entire lives."

";True. I am here to rectify that and end the enmity between us."

The viscount arched one mocking brow. "In one afternoon? Rather optimistic, wouldn't you say, my lord?"

"I may not have been a perfect father—"

The viscount let loose an explosive snort of derision.

"I may not have been a perfect father," the earl repeated patiently, "but I wanted what was best for both you and Alex."

"You had a strange way of showing it," Sebastian drawled, and slumped back into his chair.

Lord Stanhope tightened his grip on the top of his cane, his knuckles standing out in pale relief against the age-speckled skin of his hand. "You were too young to remember how your mother died. We lost her shortly after she gave birth to your sister."

Sebastian frowned. "I had a sister?"

"The babe came too early, and your mother began to bleed. There was—there was so much blood. The physician could not staunch it. I lost them both the same night."

"I never knew," Sebastian whispered.

"As she lay dying, your mother made me promise to raise you and your brother as best I could, not to relegate you to governesses and tutors but to do it myself and be involved in your lives. I fear I took her words to heart."

The viscount swallowed around his dry tongue. All he could do was nod.

"Alex was a model child. Too much so, perhaps. But where he was serious and studious, you were boisterous —forever getting into one scrape or another, falling out of trees, playing pranks.

"I had no idea how to deal with you," Lord Stanhope confessed. "My own father had barely noticed my existence, so I had no experience on which to draw. All I knew was that my life as your parent would have been easier if you had been more like Alex, so I encouraged you to follow his example."

If only you were more like your brother . . .

"You doted on Alex," the viscount stated coldly. "I always thought you loved him more than you loved me."

Lord Stanhope nodded. "I realize that now, but it was never true. I loved you, even though you were ever a contrary child. I would tell you one thing, only to have you do the exact opposite. I thought that by holding up Alex as an example you would strive to emulate him. Instead, you did everything you could to differentiate yourself."

"And it drove the two of us apart," the viscount said, scowling.

"I regret that more than you will ever know."

"Is that an apology?"

"It is, if you would accept it."

Sebastian leaned forward in his chair and propped his elbows on his knees. "And may I ask what prompted this admission?"

His father's lips compressed in a thin line, and a look of distinct discomfort crossed his face. "Before I answer that, I would ask a question of my own."

"Very well."

"When I received the note from your wife, I was quite surprised. I had heard that you would soon be engaged to her sister."

Sebastian smiled grimly. Not even his father's network of spies could have predicted what happened that night at Vauxhall. "And?" he prompted.

"I realized from the beginning what you were doing—

you sought to marry an heiress, so that you might be free of me."

What . . . ? How had he . . . ?

The viscount gaped, at a complete loss for words. He had been so sure his father would not understand what he had planned, yet the canny old devil knew everything. Damnation!

"Ask your question, my lord, and be done with it," he demanded through clenched teeth.

"In a moment—let me finish. At times you have been careless, even reckless, but I have never known you to be deliberately cruel. After what happened at Vauxhall, I could not help but think you had some feelings for the girl—otherwise you would not have done what you did and compromised her in public."

A slow, heated flush swept Sebastian's face from his chin to the top of his brow. He hated to think that his father had read him so easily, but it disturbed him even more that the earl might be right.

Why *had* he kissed Jane?

True, she had always been such fun to tease, but what happened that night went far beyond teasing. And when she had revealed that she was engaged, he could not explain the surge of anger that swept over him like a giant wave. He had found himself gripped by the overwhelming desire to protect her—to possess her. To kiss her. And clearly he had gotten carried away.

The earl broke the silence. "This is my question: do you love her?"

"You are not entitled to know my feelings, my lord," Sebastian replied. He sat up. "My marriage is none of your business."

His father held up a frail hand. "This is not about

grandchildren. I have no intention of placing any further requirements on your life."

"How generous of you. I am still struggling to deal with the ramifications of your last directive."

"When I demanded that you marry, I thought I could force you to take responsibility for your life—that I could force you to grow up. After all these years, you would think I'd have learned that I cannot force you to do anything."

"What does that mean?"

"Punish me if you must, Sebastian, but do not punish your wife. Now that you are married, you are responsible for her happiness as well as your own." The earl levered himself slowly to his feet, bracing himself against his heavy cane. "I loved your mother. You may not believe that, but I did, very much. I miss her. It's as though I lost part of myself. I came here because I do not want to see you end up as I have. Loneliness is a terrible thing, and no matter how hard you try to distract yourself, nothing seems to assuage the emptiness. But perhaps I need to let you discover this for yourself. Good-bye, my boy. I shall trouble you no further."

Sebastian rose from his seat and watched in silence as his father shuffled from the drawing room, his gait stiff and awkward. In the vestibule, the earl murmured something to Cobb. Then the front door opened and shut again.

Sebastian fell back into the chair, not trusting his knees to support him. Good God—what had just happened? He was drowning in a tumult of emotions, battered by images from both the near and distant past—his father, Alex as a boy, Alex as a man . . . and Jane, her elfin face transformed into a stony mask of hurt and distrust.

He pressed his fingers to his temples. Everything he

had ever thought about his father, every villainy Sebastian had attributed to him, flashed through his mind like a bolt of lightning. One could not undo twenty years of antipathy in a single afternoon, but the earl's words had been a revelation.

What was he supposed to do now? The man he had hated and reviled for most of his life had just apologized and confessed that he had not been a good parent. And he had revealed the circumstances that surrounded Alex's death.

He recalled so little about the day of Alex's funeral. He had been half disguised, as he had been ever since he received word of his brother's fatal accident; a haze of alcohol fogged those memories. He remembered the grief, the despair, and the sheer fury that his father had not even shown up for the funeral service. He had never thought to ask why, so wrapped up was he in his own misery. And now, to find out that his father had suffered an attack of apoplexy that left him immobilized . . . Despite his ill will toward his father, Sebastian did not wish him dead. He wished . . .

Sebastian slumped heavily against the back of his chair. He wished his father had loved him as much as he had loved Alex.

He had spent so much of his life flagrantly defying his father's wishes and flouting his authority. Making increasingly reckless wagers and flinging his roguish behavior in his father's face. And to what purpose?

The viscount threw back his head and uttered a sharp bark of laughter. His whole life had been a lie. So firmly convinced was he that his father despised him that he had made a point of provoking the earl at every turn. At the time he had thought it a fitting vengeance. Now he realized he had behaved like a sulky, recalcitrant child.

And yet, his father *had* loved him all these years, despite everything he had done. The admission rocked him to his very core. If only he had known. But the earl had been too stubborn to admit it, and Sebastian too wrapped up in his own rebellion to recognize it. What a pair of fools they had been.

Suddenly restless, Sebastian got up and paced to the sideboard. He hesitated, his hand on the stopper of the brandy decanter; then he thought the better of it. Liquor would not dull the pain, only heighten it until he collapsed in a puddle of maudlin sentiment. He needed to get out, needed to think.

He ordered his carriage brought around. He considered taking out his phaeton, but did not trust himself to handle the ribbons; he was too distracted. He ordered his baffled coachman to drive and keep driving until he told the man otherwise. Then he settled back into the shadowed interior of the carriage, one booted foot propped on the opposite bench.

The rhythmic sway of the coach calmed him, allowed him to start making sense of his jumbled thoughts.

I do not want to see you end up as I have.

He thought about his father, living day after day at cavernous Stanhope Abbey with only servants for company. He had buried one son, and the other was virtually a stranger. More than likely he had spent the past five years in that drafty mausoleum all by himself. Did he not have friends? Acquaintances? Sebastian had never considered it before.

Loneliness is a terrible thing, and no matter how hard you try to distract yourself, nothing seems to assuage the emptiness.

The viscount settled further into the plush squabs. No doubt the earl had learned about his own desperate quest for diversion; his father always seemed to know the latest gossip. In the past he had paid little attention to the earl's advice, but for some reason these words struck a chord within him. Nothing he had done in the past month satisfied him as it had before. And with Jace and Nigel absent . . . They were the only family he really had.

No, that was not true. He had Jane—his wife.

He thought about his father's query: did he love her? If by that he meant did Sebastian hold a grand passion for her, then the answer was no. She was sweet, steadfast, and possessed more intelligence and scathing wit than any other female of his acquaintance. He liked the imp. He even had a grudging respect for her. And he desired her; even now the memory of their kiss sent the blood pounding hotly through his veins.

But he did not love her. After all the rejection he had suffered in his life, both real and imagined, Sebastian did not know if he was capable of loving anyone any more. He sighed.

The rest of that conversation puzzled him. What had the earl meant when he said "do not punish her"? Was that what he was doing? She had made little secret of the fact that she despised him for what he'd done and could not wait to return to Wellbourne. And he had been just as happy to see her go, for her presence was a constant reminder of his failings.

He shifted on the padded carriage bench. Yes, she had returned home, but the gossip about her hasty marriage had likely followed her there. Her reputation might have suffered, and through it the farm as well. And the longer he remained separated from her, the worse it would become. Was he punishing her? Yes, he supposed he was.

God, he was a selfish bastard.

At least being home would provide her some consolation. What was she doing now? He stared out the window, his brows drawn in a brooding frown. Probably the same things she had always done to manage the estate. No small task, that, especially for a woman. He tried to picture his tiny wife giving orders to burly grooms and laborers; one corner of his mouth quirked at the thought.

She had never described her home to him. What was it like? He pictured a quaint brick manor house situated on a small rise and below it toward the back a large barn ringed by paddocks and pastures. Very rustic, but she had gone to great lengths to keep it. She spoke of it so fondly, like it was all she had—

Actually, it *was* all she had.

Her sister had eloped, and, if he gave any credence to Lady Portia's dire utterances, her mother had practically disowned her. All Jane had was Wellbourne.

And him.

He snorted. And a fat lot of good he had done her.

They should be content; they had each gotten what they wanted. She managed Wellbourne Grange unencumbered by an unwanted husband, while he lived the life of a wastrel here in London.

Was she as lonely as he was?

He stared out the window with hooded eyes, watching as the carriage passed a series of colorful shop fronts. With the exception of his short stay in Bath last summer, London had been his home for the past five years. He was a Corinthian, a connoisseur of London delights; he despised country life. Pride dictated he remain. But thus far pride had served him about as well as it had his father. He thought again about Jane, about her long, straight cascade of nut-brown hair, her stormy eyes . . . and her kiss.

Even when in his cups, he had not been able to shake

the memory of that kiss. She haunted him, this fey, elfin girl, the way no other woman had.

He pounded on the roof of the carriage with the head of his cane; when the coachman's concerned face appeared through the trap door, Sebastian ordered him to return home, then prepare the horses for a journey; he would leave for Leicestershire in the morning.

He needed to see Jane and to explain himself. He grimaced. That might be difficult. He barely understood the workings of his own mind—how the devil was he supposed to make *her* understand?

Only an idiot would think she would be pleased to see him; for a moment he was that idiot, then thought the better of it. After the way he had treated her, he supposed he could not blame her if she slammed the door in his face. She had every right to hate him. At any rate, he had to make the attempt. He owed her that. He just hoped that she would listen to him.

If she did not, then perhaps he would just have to stay at Wellbourne, and the two of them could be lonely together.

Chapter Eight

Jane bent over Tamerlane's muscled shoulder to dodge a few low-hanging branches as the dapple gray gelding hurtled through the last stand of trees and into the open field.

Faster, faster!

As if in response to her unspoken plea, Tam increased his stride, stretching out his neck, his black mane and tail flying like banners in the wind. Jane clung firmly to his back, her own hair loose from its pins and whipping wildly about her face. Several birds roosting in a hedge objected to their thunderous passing and took flight in a great flurry of feathers. Both horse and rider ignored them.

Tam sailed over a stone wall as effortlessly as if he had sprouted wings of his own, then landed and resumed his lightning pace, his hooves pounding against the dense, springy turf. Sweat darkened his neck and withers. Jane knew she should be heading back to the stables, but still she rode as if demons pursued her.

Well, not demons. Not exactly. Just the knowledge that some day, without warning, all of this could be ripped away from her, and she would be powerless to stop it.

Try as she might, she could not leave the thought behind. It was no use running. She reined in the big gelding. Tamerlane snorted a protest and danced sideways.

Jane chuckled. "You old reprobate. You would run your heart out if I let you, and I have no intention of doing that. We have galloped every day since we got home, and we shall do it again tomorrow. Now, behave yourself."

The horse's ears swiveled at the sound of her voice. He stamped his off hind foot, sidled a bit more, then obeyed and settled down to a walk. Jane smiled and patted his neck.

Movement caught her eye as she reached the top of a hill. A cloud of dust rose from the direction of the road. Shielding her eyes against the glare of the sun, Jane stretched upward to get a better look.

A carriage drawn by two high-stepping blacks made its way down the lane toward Wellbourne. Jane frowned. That couldn't be Lord Erskine; the Scottish earl was not due for another three days. Who, then? At this distance, she could not make out the crest emblazoned on the side of the coach. Not that it mattered. Wellbourne received so few visitors these days that any arrival made her sit up and take notice.

She ran a hand over her wild tangle of hair. Gracious! It would not do for her guest to see her looking like this. If she moved quickly enough, she might be able to reach the house before he did. She turned Tamerlane for home and nudged him into a canter.

"A caller's come for you, Miss Jane," Will said as she returned to the main stable.

Mr. Finley, Wellbourne's steward, emerged from the row of box stalls, leading a bay mare. "She's Lady Langley now, you nob," he corrected with a scowl. "Have some respect."

Jane shook her head. "Never mind, Mr. Finley. I see no reason to trouble myself with such formalities." She dismounted and handed the reins to the groom. "Do you know who it is, Will?"

The man tugged at his forelock. "Some fancy lord from Lunnon, Miss Jane. That's all I know."

"Well, then, let us hope he's rich and looking for several new hunters," she replied, smiling.

She hurried toward the house, her riding crop gripped between her teeth so that she could use both hands to smooth her hair into some semblance of order. A few pins still remained; she fashioned a makeshift chignon and hoped it stayed anchored long enough for her to greet her guest.

When she reached the cool interior of the house, the butler took her gloves and riding crop. Concern lined the servant's craggy face.

Jane paused. "What is it, Huxley?"

"A visitor for you, ma'am," the man said. He presented her with a calling card. "He is waiting in the drawing room. Shall I inform him you are at home?"

She glanced down at the cream-colored card. The printed name leaped out at her like an adder made of black ink.

Sebastian Carr, Viscount Langley.

She gasped. The card slipped from her fingers and fluttered to the floor.

"Miss Jane? Are you well?" Huxley inquired. His anxious eyes regarded her from beneath bushy, snow-white brows.

Jane put a hand to her throat; beneath her fingers, her pulse beat at a frantic pace. She swallowed. He had been bound to come, and now that he was here she suspected that he would not be put off for long. She must face him sooner or later.

She straightened. "I am fine. Is he alone?"

"Yes, ma am."

Thank God for that! "Good. Tell him I shall be with him directly."

The servant hesitated. "Miss Jane?"

"Yes?"

"Forgive my impertinence, ma'am, but is he . . . ?"

Jane's lips curved in a mirthless smile. "Yes, Huxley. He is my husband."

Flustered, the butler bowed and retreated.

Jane glared at the card lying so innocuously on the in-laid wooden floor. So much for leaving her in peace. Her knees began to shake. How much had he lost? Was he here to tell her that she no longer had a home, that he'd gambled everything away? Or did he want to take inventory of the horses before he auctioned them at Tattersall's?

Or did he intend to consummate their marriage?

She leaned against a gilt-edged table in the hall for support until the dizziness passed, then put a hand to her side and took several deep, steadying breaths. Whatever his reason, he might at least have written to give her some warning. This was too sudden. She was not ready . . .

She clenched her jaw, furious at him for arriving without notice, and furious at herself for letting him upset her. This was *her* home. He was the interloper. How dare he come here and cut up her peace!

Fortified by anger, Jane lifted her chin and marched toward the drawing room.

She paused when she reached the threshold and stared. The viscount stood at the window, his back to her, looking out toward the south pasture. The late afternoon sun slanted through the windows and glinted off his hair, giving it a rich golden glow. In this light, he almost looked like an angel. She harrumphed. An angel? Not likely!

He turned at the sound, and Jane's heart tumbled over in her chest. The sight of him made her as lightheaded as if she'd had one too many glasses of champagne. A lock of his hair had fallen over his eyes, and she felt a sudden, inexplicable urge to reach up and brush it away. Her gaze lingered on his mouth; though she had tried her best to forget, the memory of their kiss came flooding back.

She licked her suddenly dry lips.

His slate blue gaze locked to hers. "Good day, wife," he said softly.

The warmth in his voice made her shiver. Damn him! She would not let him take advantage of her weakness again.

"What are you doing here?" she demanded.

"What, not even so much as a 'good afternoon'? You wound me, madam." A teasing smile quirked one corner of his expressive mouth.

"Did you expect a cordial welcome? You send no word of your arrival but simply show up on my doorstep unannounced and uninvited. You cannot be surprised that I am somewhat less than overjoyed to see you."

His smile faded. "I suspected you might be."

"What brings you to Wellbourne Grange?" She swallowed thickly, then steeled herself for the answer.

"Egad, imp, you've gone pale as a ghost. Perhaps you had better sit down."

"Not until you give me an answer."

Comprehension shadowed his eyes. "Nothing is wrong, if that is what you mean," he replied in a quiet voice. "Wellbourne is in no danger."

Relief rushed through Jane in a giddy wave; she sagged against the doorframe.

The viscount frowned, then started across the room toward her, one arm outstretched.

She held up a warning hand. "Thank you, but I can manage quite well without your assistance."

He lowered his arm. "So I see."

She squared her shoulders and paced to the mantelpiece. "If Wellbourne is in no danger, then you should not have come."

"Why not?"

"I thought that would be obvious, my lord. I do not want you here."

He spread his hands. "But I am here, and I should hate to have wasted a trip."

"If you need to discuss matters of business, then you should take your concerns to my solicitor."

"I did not want to speak to your solicitor. I wanted to see you."

"Well, now you have seen me. You can return to London safe in the knowledge that I have not been trampled or robbed, and that I suffer from no ailments, including heartbreak."

He shoved a hand through his hair, rumpling the golden brown waves. "I cannot return to London just yet. We need to talk."

"I cannot imagine that we would have anything of importance to say to each other," she said pettishly.

He stalked across the Turkey carpet toward her. "Perhaps you have nothing to say to me, but there are a great many things I wish to tell you. Now will you stop arching your back and hissing at me long enough to listen?"

She gaped at him. Arching her . . . ? A furious blush lit her cheeks, and she snapped her mouth shut, piqued.

"Thank you." He moved to stand at the other end of the mantel, out of reach, but not far enough away for comfort. "My father came to see me two days ago."

Jane favored him with a narrow, guarded glance.

He did not seem to notice. "We have reconciled, after a fashion. Perhaps *reconciled* is the wrong word; it will take more than a single conversation to mend the rift between us. But we have begun to understand each other. It was a very . . . enlightening conversation."

Questions roiled in Jane's mind, but she had promised to keep silent, so she merely folded her arms over her chest and waited.

"We are stubborn idiots, my father and I. Once we fix on an idea, we hold onto it like a dog with a particularly juicy bone and refuse to let it go. For my father, it was the idea that he could force me into taking greater responsibility for myself. For me, it was . . . Well, I realized that I have been an ass on a number of occasions. In fact, I have been an ass most of my life."

Jane flashed him a fair imitation of her mother's best, most supercilious "oh, really?" look.

He shifted uneasily. "But the main reason for his visit was to discuss you and me, and our marriage."

The words burst out before she could stop them. "We have no marriage, my lord."

"No, we do not. And I would like to rectify that situation."

She stiffened. "What did you have in mind?"

"You may not believe this, but I have grown rather weary of life in London. With Jace on his honeymoon and Nigel gone to ground somewhere, my favorite pastimes have lost their appeal."

"You are quite right," she replied. "I do not believe it."

She expected him to chastise her for lashing her tail as

well, but instead, he chuckled. "My father likes you, you know."

"Really? How extraordinary."

"He says you have pluck."

She nudged one of the andirons with the toe of her boot. "That is one way to phrase it." Hissing, indeed!

"But my presence here owes more to you than anything else."

She frowned. "To me? What do you mean?"

"I wanted to see you. I wanted to visit Wellbourne and discover why you went to such great lengths to preserve it. I thought we might . . . reconsider our arrangement."

"Did your father suggest this?" she demanded.

"No. This was solely my idea."

"Then the earl has placed no . . . demands upon us?"

The viscount shook his head. "Nothing of the sort. If it is any consolation, I am as shocked as you are that he has not."

"I see." Actually, Jane did *not* see. What was really going on? She had heard him speak of country life with marked distaste, and suddenly he wished to rusticate with her on a stud farm in Leicestershire? Something did not seem right. "And how long do you plan to stay, my lord?"

"I had not planned much beyond my arrival," he replied with a slight smile. "I suspected you might wish to throw me out. But if I am safe on that account, I would like to stay a month or two. I hope that will not inconvenience you."

Well, there was one way to find out if he was telling the truth. "Not at all, my lord. As a matter of fact, we could use the help."

His smile evaporated. "Help?"

"Yes. One of the grooms broke his leg in a fall from one of the haylofts, and we are short-handed at the moment. How very generous of you to offer your assistance."

It took all the self-control at her command not to laugh as she watched the play of emotions over Lord Langley's face. If he really wanted to learn more about her and about Wellbourne, she could think of no better way than to let him discover firsthand how much work the estate entailed. She could hardly imagine the elegant viscount, whose hands had never toiled with anything heavier than a deck of cards, mucking out stalls or wrestling to get a halter on a fractious one-year-old colt. He would never even consider such a thing, she was sure of it, and he would be on his merry way back to London in the morning.

"All right," he agreed.

Her jaw sagged.

Lord Langley grinned. "You seem surprised. You forget that I am a veteran gamester. I know when someone is bluffing."

Bluffing, was she? Jane smiled sweetly at him. "One thing you will learn about me, my lord, is that I never bluff. I will see to it that your things are installed in one of the guest chambers. We keep country hours here, so I will instruct someone to wake you at an hour past sunrise every morning. After all, we do not have the luxury of sleeping until noon." She started toward the doorway.

His resonant chuckle rippled like water over velvet. "Try what you will, wife, but you cannot drive me off so easily."

"We shall see about that," she muttered.

What had he done?

Sebastian groaned. The plaguey imp would have made one of the best Captain Sharps of his acquaintance; she had gulled him like a green youth. He had been so certain that she had been bluffing, but she'd played her hand to the hilt.

As she had promised, one of the maids, a perky red-headed creature called Meg, had roused him at an ungodly early hour, informing him that Miss Jane needed him down in the main stable. He had uttered a blistering oath, then buried himself under the covers. Meg had persisted, puttering about his room while humming an off-key ditty, flinging open the curtains so the morning sun streamed through his east-facing window, until he could not take the torture any more. With a roar he had flung himself out of bed. He probably should have warned poor little Meg in advance that he slept in nothing but what God had given him; she had taken one look at his naked form, gasped in dismay, and fled.

He may have won that battle, but the war had only just begun. It had not taken him long at all to realize that the entire staff at Wellbourne, from the scullery maids to the coachman, knew who he was, and what he had done to "their Miss Jane." Most of them, though properly polite and deferential, succeeded in making him feel like an unwanted intruder; conversations stopped mid-sentence at his approach, followed by stretches of glacial silence. Will, the head groom, took particular delight in giving him the dirtiest, most back-breaking jobs in the stable. After a week of doing nothing but mucking out stalls, Sebastian had little to show for it but a few blisters, a sunburn, and wretchedly aching muscles.

But he was not going to throw in his cards yet and admit that a slip of a girl and her servants had gotten the better of him. Although he resented the hard work, after a few days he found that he was beginning to enjoy it— once the worst of the aches had subsided, that is. He had not touched a drop of anything stronger than Madeira in days and no longer woke each morning with a muzzy head. His body had begun to adapt; his muscles were beginning to harden and no longer protested with such vehemence when he picked up a pitchfork. His head seemed clearer, his mind sharper, than it had been in years.

And he would never have suspected that he would develop an affinity for the Leicestershire countryside. The slight breeze that ruffled his hair this morning smelled of freshly turned earth and new-mown hay, rather than the coal smoke and the stench of the Thames that hung heavily over the streets of London. Birdsong caroled from nearly every tree and hedge, far preferable to the constant cries of street vendors and the noisy rumble of cart and carriage wheels on cobbled streets. Dew lay heavy on the grass, gilded to a diamond brightness by the mid-morning sun. He could not remember the last time he had seen dew in London.

Most importantly of all, he was beginning to learn a great deal about his wife. Although she had a small army of servants to run Wellbourne, she walked down to the stables every morning, going first to Mr. Finley's office, then talking with the grooms and wandering down the rows of box stalls, giving a pat or a handful of oats to the horses lodged there. She spoke with Wellbourne's head trainer, Mr. Monk, about the progress of their young horses. She inspected the paddocks and fences, then issued any necessary instructions; every man, from the most hulking laborer to the smallest stable boy, treated the tiny "Miss Jane" with the utmost respect. At first he had been piqued that no one referred to her as Lady Langley, but it made sense. Jane did not want the title any more than she had wanted this marriage.

In the afternoon, she would retreat back to the Jacobean style manor house, a lovely red brick construction ornamented with gables, turrets, and dozens of mullioned windows, to keep the accounts and greet callers from the neighborhood. After three o'clock she would don her dark green riding habit and mount Tamerlane, her long-legged gray gelding, and disappear into the fields at a breakneck gallop.

By the time the two of them sat down for dinner at opposite ends of the massive dining table, both were usually too tired to keep up much of a conversation. Which was just as well, he supposed—since he had come to Wellbourne, Jane had not shown much enthusiasm for talking to him at all. What they did manage to say to each other was stilted and awkward, at best.

Working in the stables had given him a unique perspective of her life and the people who shared it. While her employees doted on her with the familiarity of long-standing service, the local gentry showed her no such kindness. He ascertained that Mrs. Wingate, the mother of Jane's nearest neighbor, and Lady Ainsley, the wife of the local baronet, were the worst. These two tabbies were responsible for the gossip running rampant, most of it about Jane, yet still they had the temerity to call on her and offer their sympathies for her plight. Sympathies— bah. He would wager they kept coming for the express purpose of finagling more information out of Jane, which they would then turn around and use against her. Sebastian found himself gritting his teeth whenever he spied either lady's carriage coming up the drive.

He had attempted to talk to Jane after their latest visit, but she remained pale and tight-lipped.

"They came to spew their usual venom, my lord," she said dismissively. "Lady Ainsley in particular was a bosom-bow of my mother, so you would think I should be immune to such hypocrisy and ill will."

"But I can see it still pains you," he replied in a quiet voice. "Why have you told no one but your staff about my presence here? It might spare you any further distress."

She turned on him, the stormy shade of her eyes a match for her thunderous expression. "And what will they say when you leave for London and do not return? It will only make matters worse. I do not need you to protect me, my lord."

She strode away, her entire body stiff with outrage. He watched her go, fighting back his own anger. She did not need him? From what he had seen, she did not need anyone. She kept herself aloof and detached, immersing herself in the daily management of Wellbourne. Perhaps he had been mistaken; the imp was not lonely, after all. She was too busy to feel lonely—or feel much of anything, for that matter.

Exasperated, he stalked back down to the stables, picked up his pitchfork, and started in on the next stall with an excess of anger-fed energy. She did not need him. He tossed a forkful of soiled straw into the wheelbarrow. She did not need anyone. And she had simply assumed that he would return to London without a second thought. His coming to Wellbourne in the first place, his tolerance of being treated like a servant, all meant nothing to her. Damned irritating creature. Maddening, headstrong, stubborn, plaguesome . . . Forkful after forkful of straw went into the wheelbarrow with each word; he ran out of bedding before he ran out of epithets.

He leaned on his pitchfork, breathing hard from exertion. "Do not punish her," his father had said. Punish her? 'Twas *she* who was punishing *him*! He had come here to

mend his fences with her—devil take it, he had even
agreed to do manual labor, of all things!—but she remained as unyielding and unforgiving as ever.

He had had enough. Come morning, he would pack up
his things and return to London. Like a petulant child, she
had done nothing but turn up her nose at his every over-
ture of goodwill. He'd be damned if he'd stay here and
make an even greater fool of himself.

He set his pitchfork aside and wandered out into the
passageway between the rows of box stalls, kicking at the
loose straw that littered the ground. Several horses stuck
out their heads as he did so, their ears pricked forward. A
blaze-faced bay whickered softly at him.

"Easy there, my girl," he murmured, and gently
rubbed at the whorl of hair on the horse's broad forehead.
He *would* miss this; he had grown fond of these beasts,
this sweet-natured bay mare in particular. He had not
been in the saddle since his own mare had pulled up
lame, and that was over a month ago. Before he left, perhaps he could convince Mr. Finley to let him take this
lady out for a brief gallop.

A noise distracted him. What was that? He cocked an
ear. It sounded for all the world like a woman sobbing.
No, he must be mistaken. A woman, in the stables? Jane
was still up at the house. Must be one of the maids. Or
was it?

Curious, Sebastian gave the bay mare a last, absent
pat, then walked slowly toward the source of the sound.
In the last stall, a small figure in a green riding habit
leaned against Tamerlane's withers, her arms thrown
around the horse's neck, sobbing as if her heart were broken.

"Jane?" he asked softly.

She gasped, then quickly ducked her head and brushed

the tears from her face. "I—I did not see you standing there, my lord," she stammered.

"So I noticed." He had learned early on in his labors that a jacket and waistcoat only got in the way when mucking out stalls; he stood before her in his shirtsleeves, his collar open at the throat, without even so much as a handkerchief to offer her.

Her hands shaking, she daubed at the lingering moisture with the cuff of one sleeve. "I suppose you would not believe me if I said I had something in my eye."

"I would believe whatever you cared to tell me," he replied in the gentlest tone at his command.

A fresh wave of moisture glittered on her lashes; she quickly blotted it away. "I . . . wanted to get away from the house for a time."

Apparently she was not immune to the harpies' venom. The thought heartened him. Maybe she *did* need someone, after all.

He stepped closer and stroked the gray's neck. "I will wager this fellow makes a very good listener."

That earned him a watery smile. "He does. He never passes judgment, never gossips, and never interrupts."

The gelding snuffled him, then lipped at his sleeve.

"He is a fine horse," Sebastian commented. "I first admired him when we met in Hyde Park, but upon closer inspection he is nothing short of magnificent. If you had another like him, I would snap him up in an instant."

"Then I fear you would have to wait a rather long time," she said. "Most of our most promising three- and four-year-olds have already been purchased in preparation for the next hunting season. We have a few older horses that my father bred, but I cannot bring myself to part with them."

"You must miss him very much."

"More than you can imagine." Her tentative smile faded. The gray nickered and nudged at her shoulder. "The farm will never be the same without him, and although I do my best to manage things as he would have wanted, we are not doing as well as I should like; gentlemen are not accustomed to purchasing their hunters from a lady."

"I wish you would let me help you," he murmured.

She averted her gaze and reached up to twirl a lock of the gelding's mane between her fingers. "Do you know how my father died, my lord?"

"I confess I do not."

A single, silvery tear trailed down her cheek. "Papa was one of the most even-tempered men in the world; rarely did anything trouble him. Except, that is, for my mother and her constant carping. You see, breeding horses for the hunt may be a genteel occupation, but it is too close to trade for a high stickler like her. No matter how hard my father tried to please her, nothing was ever good enough—not the renovations to the manor house, not her wardrobe full of fashionable clothes, not her case full of jewels." Bitterness limned her words.

"Go on," he coaxed.

"About three years ago she began to visit London for weeks at a time. She told my father that she went to visit a cousin of hers who was feeling poorly and needed her care."

Sebastian raised an eyebrow. Never in his brief acquaintance with Lady Portia had he known the woman to care for anyone but herself.

"My father may have been a mere 'Honorable,' my lord, but he was not blind, nor was he a fool. He knew exactly what she was doing, and it crushed him. He loved my mother. I cannot explain why, but he did.

"Soon after he made that discovery, he took to the bottle. Not that I noticed, at first, but gradually he began to drink so much that he could not rise before noon, and some days he could not get out of bed at all."

"So you stood in for him," Sebastian guessed.

She nodded. "Mama would not. Pen could not. I was the only one left."

"How old were you?"

"Sixteen."

Sebastian muttered a hot, utterly scathing imprecation beneath his breath.

"But I was not alone—not entirely," she hastened to add. "Mr. Finley saw what was happening, too, and did what he could to help, although we were not able to conceal the problem from the staff for long. In the end, the servants knew to come to me instead of my father."

The viscount's fingers tightened into a fist. Heat sizzled through his veins. What sort of man relied on his schoolroom-aged daughter to run his estate? And what sort of mother allowed it to happen? Small wonder the imp was so serious; she had had responsibility thrust upon her at an early age. "How long did this go on?"

"A year, perhaps a little longer; I lost track of time after a while. The stables began to suffer as fewer and fewer gentlemen wanted to deal with my father."

"That must have been very painful for you to watch."

"It was. Then one night my father decided he wanted to ride Pharaoh, one of our young stallions. Drinking made him belligerent, and he was already half-seas over. A few of the grooms tried to stop him but could not. Will still bears a scar from where my father struck him with his riding crop."

"What happened, Jane?" he asked softly.

"Pharaoh was young and not used to being manhandled, much less whipped. He threw my father, then trampled him before we could pull him away."

Sebastian felt the blood drain from his face. "God in heaven."

"Papa was dead, and we had to put Pharaoh down that same night. When I woke my mother and told her what had happened, she simply shrugged and said, 'It was bound to happen,' then went back to bed. Bound to happen! She felt no remorse. None at all." Her voice trembled with anger.

"Do you hate her so much?"

"My mother cannot change what she is, my lord," she replied in strangled tones. "Do you hate the wasp because it stings?"

"But you blame her for his death."

"Yes. Yes, I suppose I do. But my father shares an equal portion of the blame for choosing to hide from his problems at the bottom of a bottle."

Sophisticated charmer though he was, Sebastian could find no glib words to smooth over the raw emotion that hung heavy in the air. He swallowed around the ache at the back of his throat. "I'm sorry."

She stroked the gray's muscular shoulder. "You need not be. We are managing, though we have not had an easy time of it. Tamerlane here is Pharaoh's half brother, and he seemed promising as a stud, but his temperament proved too hot and we had to geld him. I can only hope this year's crop of colts will compensate for the loss."

In spite of himself, Sebastian winced and skewed a sideways glance at the horse. "Bad luck, old chap," he muttered, then turned his attention back to Jane. "Why did you not tell me any of this?"

"I—I did not think you cared to know."

He placed his hands on her shoulders and gave them a

gentle squeeze. "That is why I am here, in case you had not noticed. I came to further our acquaintance."

"Perhap . . ." She hesitated, then started to pull away.

He kept his grip gentle, but firm; he was not about to let her run away now, not when she had just started to open up to him. "Perhaps what?"

"Perhaps that is not such a good idea."

He frowned. "What are you saying?"

She seized her lower lip between her teeth and looked up at him, her eyes anguished. "My father loved my mother, but received nothing but her indifference in return. Some might say that hate is the opposite of love, but I cannot agree with that. Hate is a powerful emotion, and thus something one can understand or at least accept for what it is. To my way of thinking, indifference is a complete lack of love—a complete lack of any feeling at all. My father could not understand my mother's apathy, and eventually it destroyed him. I will not allow history to repeat itself."

His frown deepened. "What do you mean?"

"Do you love me, my lord?"

Her question nearly stopped his heart. "Jane, I do not think—"

"Do you?"

He met her searching gaze. "How can I, when you have never given me the chance?"

She blinked several times in rapid succession, and a faint hint of color stole into her cheeks. "I am not one of those young ladies who spends the entire day reading Minerva Press romances," she said hurriedly. "I am not so foolish as to think love is all-encompassing, nor that it is a magic spell that can make all our difficulties disappear. But without it, and without trust, I fear our marriage has no hope of success, and we may as well continue to lead separate lives."

"I have no hope of developing any feelings for you when you insist on keeping me at a distance," he replied. "All I ask is that you give me the opportunity to undo the cruel things I have done to you."

She continued to try to pull away from him, lines of uncertainty creasing her brow. "I want to trust you, my lord, but—"

"I seem to recall a night in London when I asked you to say my name," he said, his voice a throaty murmur. "I enjoyed hearing you say it then, and I would enjoy it all the more now."

Her blush burst into full bloom across her high, angled cheekbones. "Sebastian."

A little thrill coursed down his spine. "There. Was that so bad?"

"No."

"Then I encourage you to use it as often as you'd like."

"Why did you kiss me that night at Vauxhall?" she blurted out.

Sebastian hesitated. Why had he, indeed? He exhaled in a slow sigh. "Because I wanted to," he replied. And he realized that was the perfect truth.

"Not to punish me or teach me a lesson?" she whispered.

"No. Just to kiss you." He took a step closer to her. "As a matter of fact, I would very much like to do it again, if you will allow me."

"I—I don't . . ."

But she did not move, so he placed a hand beneath her chin and leaned down. "Give me a chance," he breathed.

She closed her eyes.

He kissed each corner of her mouth, then brushed his

lips over hers like butterfly wings. Nothing more than that, for now. He had no wish to frighten her and undo everything he'd accomplished this afternoon. He suspected that the time for passionate, devouring, all-consuming kisses would come soon enough.

He raised his head. "Give me the chance to love you, Jane."

She opened her eyes and stared up at him. She gave a convulsive swallow. "Very well, Sebastian. I will try."

Chapter Nine

What had she done?

Jane's head spun with the ramifications of what had happened yesterday afternoon. Instead of giving up and going back to London, as she had foolishly hoped, the viscount had asked for permission to court her. And she was going to let him.

Part of her wanted to climb up into the haymow and hide. That may have worked when she was eight and sought to avoid her mother's wrath, but she was eighteen, almost nineteen, and married. As much as she disliked the thought, she had a duty to her husband, and she could not hide from him forever.

He was sincere about his offer to make amends; she was sure of that now. Why else had he endured over a fortnight of menial, backbreaking labor in her stables? Guilt pricked her for treating him so abominably, especially since he had done the work without complaint. She had behaved like a petulant child, and she was more than a little ashamed of herself.

Dared she hope that something good would come of the viscount's stay at Wellbourne? He had a way with horses; she could see it in the way he treated the animals and the way they responded to his light touch. Her father had never believed in training horses with brute force but preferred gentler methods. Her husband appeared to share those sentiments.

Her husband.

Jane shivered as she donned the jacket of her riding habit. The word still sounded so strange, even after all these weeks. Her husband. Sebastian.

What was he up to? He had asked her to dress for riding and meet him in the stables this afternoon but, with a wicked twinkle in his slate blue eyes, refused to tell her why. Incorrigible man. The very prospect of meeting him in the stables again made her fingers tremble so that she could barely button up her jacket.

Gracious, she was behaving like a complete scatterbrain, rather like Penelope did before her come-out ball. Jane's fingers stilled over the last set of buttons. Dear Pen. She felt her sister's absence more keenly now that Lord Langley—Sebastian—had come to stay at Wellbourne. She longed to be able to go to the room across the hall, sit on her sister's bed, and ask Pen for advice. Knowing Pen, she might not have gotten much in the way of guidance, but her sister had always been willing to listen while Jane poured out her heart. Fledgling tears swelled at the back of her throat. Dearest Pen—how much she missed her!

Jane closed the last button and tugged at her jacket. A small sad smile tipped her lips. Even though her sister was miles away, Jane knew exactly what Pen would tell her: make a list.

She glanced at the escritoire in the corner of her bedchamber. Why not? She had a few minutes before she had to meet Sebastian.

She sat down at the little writing desk and took out a sheet of parchment, then dipped her pen in the inkwell.

Merits, she wrote in a bold hand.

Beneath it, she wrote the following items, each with its own comment:

Handsome—yes, well, that much was established from the start.

Charming—too much so, perhaps. How much is flummery; how much is sincere?

Sense of humor—he seems to use it mostly to tease me.

Honorable—he did marry me.

Passionate—

Jane paused, her pen poised above the paper. Though the kiss he had given her yesterday was sweet and chaste, she knew from that night at Vauxhall that his kisses could be very, very passionate indeed. The tips of her ears grew warm.

She shook herself and took out a second sheet of parchment. At the top of this page she wrote *Shortcomings*.

Mercenary—wanted to marry Pen for her money.

Gamester—too fond of gambling, according to gossip; claims that he has reformed.

Untrustworthy—??; has proven himself reliable since his arrival at Wellbourne.

Dislikes the country—although he does not seem unhappy here.

Execrable taste in friends—if I ever see Lord Nigel Barrington again, I will take a pitchfork to his backside!

Then, at the bottom of both lists, she added one more entry: *I love him.*

She stared at those three words. It was true; she did still love him. Over the past month she had tried to forget him, tried to forget her feelings for him, and cursed herself for her inability to do either. He had hurt her cruelly and still she loved him. She was either the world's greatest fool or its greatest idealist. Thus, the entry on both lists.

Six merits, six drawbacks. Although it came down to one issue and one alone: Did she trust him? She put the pen back in its holder, capped the inkwell, and sighed. Lists may have made Pen feel better, but they did little for her.

A light rap on the door startled her; she jumped. "Sebastian?"

The door opened. Meg stood in the doorway, her face pale beneath her flaming red hair.

"What is it, Meggie?" Jane asked, frowning.

"Mr. Augustus Wingate is downstairs for you, Miss Jane, an' he don't look too happy. Says he has an urgent matter to discuss."

Jane cringed. She had not seen her neighbor since her return to Wellbourne. To tell the truth, she had dreaded ever encountering her former fiancé again. Now it seemed that Augustus had taken the decision out of her hands.

"Thank you, Meg," she said with a nod.

The maid curtsied and vanished.

Jane saw no reason to delay the inevitable. She rose from her escritoire, rubbed her palms against her skirts, and headed for the stairs. She had no idea what sort of "urgent matter" brought Augustus to Wellbourne, but she hoped the visit would not take long; she had promised to meet Sebastian in a matter of minutes.

When she entered the drawing room, she saw Augustus standing before the window, much as Sebastian had upon his arrival. She could not help but compare the two. Before their trip to London, Jane had thought their neighbor fairly young; now, in the bright afternoon light, she could detect the tracery of lines around Augustus's eyes and mouth—he appeared well over forty. An unhealthy flush mottled his cheeks. Though he had always had a tendency to be stout, he had gained weight in the past few months; his belly strained the buttons of his brown and tan striped waistcoat, and his russet coat fit rather badly about the shoulders. In a nod to current fashion, he had combed his thick brown hair into the fashionable Brutus style. High, sharp collar points and an intricately tied cravat framed his receding double chin. From a ribbon around his neck dangled a quizzing glass on a ribbon, which he twirled in his fingers.

She cleared her throat. "Good afternoon, Mr. Wingate."

He swiveled around to face her, quizzing glass raised. Jane found herself being scrutinized from head to toe like a horse at auction. What, did he expect her to open her mouth so he might inspect her teeth? She raised her chin and stared reprovingly back at him.

"You are looking as well as ever, Miss Jane," he commented at length, lowering his glass. "But I suppose I should address you as Lady Langley. I have not yet had the opportunity to offer you my felicitations on your marriage."

"Thank you, Mr. Wingate," she replied. She forced herself to relax, then gestured to one of the more sturdy chairs by the hearth. "Do sit down."

"Ever the generous hostess." The hint of a sneer curled the man's lips. "Unfortunately, I cannot stay long, so I shall come directly to the purpose of my visit."

"And what would that be, Mr. Wingate?"

He let fall the quizzing glass, then clasped his hands behind his back, which made his newly acquired paunch protrude all the more. "There was a time, dearest Jane, when you called me by my Christian name."

"I . . . regret the way matters ended between us."

Beneath his dark brows, Mr. Wingate's pale gray eyes glittered with something Jane could not identify. It made her shiver.

"Do you, my dear?" he asked in a mocking tone. "You are now a viscountess, the wife of the heir to the Earl of Stanhope. I cannot imagine why you would think that preferable to a marriage with me."

"I did not go to London with the intention of jilting you," Jane replied hotly.

"No, of course not." His tone made the words an insult.

She stiffened. "If you have come for no reason but to slight me, sirrah, then I must bid you good day."

"Slight you? Jane, how could you think such a thing? I have given you no greater offense than your husband has. He *is* still in London, I assume? Does he even remember that you exist?"

"I suggest you come to the point, Mr. Wingate," she snapped.

"My point is, sweet Jane, that you should have married me."

"And as I told you in my letter, sir, circumstances made marriage between us impossible."

He waggled a finger at her. "Be that as it may, we had a prior agreement that you were obliged to honor."

"I had no choice but to wed Lord Langley."

A look of smug satisfaction illumined the man's round face. "I disagree, my dear. You agreed to marry me, but then you threw me over for another more likely prospect. And so you give me no other recourse but to sue you for breach of promise."

Jane's eyes saucered. *"What?"*

"You heard correctly, sweeting." He gestured to the room. "All of this should have been mine—it would have been, had you not fallen under Viscount Langley's spell."

"But we were never formally engaged," she protested.

"You made a promise to me, but you went back on your word. You left me little choice. Oh, you need not worry about keeping Wellbourne itself—I fear that now belongs to your husband. But if my case is successful, and I am certain it will be, you shall be obliged to pay me what this estate is worth, in addition to compensation commensurate with my injured feelings. I want only what is due me."

Jane felt the blood drain from her face. "You cannot do this."

He arched a mocking brow. "Can I not?" Then he paused. "Of course, if you are amenable, we might be able to settle this matter ourselves and never bring it to the attention of the law."

"What do you have in mind?" Jane ventured, though she dreaded the answer.

"Well, to begin with, I want you to deed to me the stretch of pasture closest to my lands."

She shook her head. "I cannot. That field has a stream running through it. The horses need the water at this time of year."

"Then you can lease it back from me."

"For an exorbitant amount of money, I will wager."

He smirked. "Oh, not that exorbitant. And there is one more thing."

"What?" she asked from between clenched teeth.

"I shall also require the sum of five hundred pounds a month in return for my silence. After all, sweeting, your reputation can scarcely afford another scandal. Why, if word were to reach the Duke of Rutland or any other arbiters of the hunt, Wellbourne would be ruined."

Five hundred pounds a month? That translated to six thousand pounds a year—a small fortune!

"This is blackmail," Jane said flatly. "I cannot possibly afford to pay you that much."

"Of course you can," he crooned. His smile widened. "You have a wealthy husband, Jane. Surely you can think of something."

Cold, she felt so cold. A shiver crawled down her spine. "Why are you doing this, Augustus? I thought you were a decent man."

"I *am* a decent man, my dear," he replied, still smirking. "That is why I came to you first. Only a bounder of the first order would have brought suit without warning."

"I see." Jane snapped her arms around herself. "I—I will need some time to consider your offer."

Wingate's smirk faded; he pursed his lips, then consulted his pocket timepiece. "You have until nine o'clock this evening, Lady Langley—not enough time to petition your husband in London, so I beg you to discard any such foolish notions. Besides, if any of what I hear is to be believed, he would not help you anyway."

Jane's horrified gaze flicked to the clock on the mantelpiece. "Nine o'clock? But that is scarcely six hours!"

"Nine o'clock. After that I take no responsibility for what may happen." Her neighbor stuffed his watch back into his waistcoat, inclined his head in the briefest of nods, and sauntered from the room.

Jane's legs gave way beneath her, and she sagged heavily onto the striped divan. How could she have ever considered marriage to that—that greedy, overfed lout? And to think that he had the gall to blackmail her, then claim he was doing her a favor!

Breach of promise. She had not even considered this as a consequence of her marriage to Sebastian. Wellbourne could not afford any more scandal—but could it afford the terms of Augustus's extortion? And even if she did manage to pay him, nothing could stop him from demanding more money or more land. She squeezed her eyes shut and balled her hands into fists. What was she going to do? Her previous engagement to Augustus had been a sore point with Sebastian. What was she going to tell him?

"Jane?"

A constricted squeak escaped Jane's throat, and she shot to her feet.

Sebastian ambled into the drawing room, wearing boots, breeches, a fine lawn shirt, and a wicked grin. His white teeth gleamed against his tanned skin.

"There you are! I was beginning to think you had forgotten about our afternoon ride." His gaze searched her face, and his smile faded. "Was that Mrs. Wingate's carriage I saw leaving just now? You are so pale. Did she upset you?"

Jane shook her head. "No. Not Mrs. Wingate. Her son, Augustus. My former fiancé."

"What did he want?" Sebastian asked, his eyes narrowed in suspicion.

"I—that is—he—" Try as she might, she could not

force the words out. Tears of anger and frustration welled within her.

The viscount crossed to the sideboard in several swift strides; he poured a glass of sherry, then pressed it into her hand. "Here. Drink this."

Jane took a large sip. The sherry flooded her tongue with a heady liquid warmth

"Slowly," Sebastian counseled. "Now, what happened?"

Would he believe her innocent of any fault? She had no way to know unless she told him. Jane took a deep breath.

"He said he intends to sue me for breach of promise."

"Breach of promise?" Sebastian repeated, his brows drawn in an angry line. "He would not dare."

"He would," Jane said miserably. "He offered for me because he wanted Wellbourne, and now that he's been thwarted, he wants compensation."

"Like hell he does."

She nodded. "But he has offered to keep this out of the courts. For a price."

"Has he? What does he want?"

"The pasture that borders hard by his lands and five hundred pounds a month."

"That's blackmail."

"I know."

"And if we do not pay him?"

He had said "we," not "you." A ray of hope pierced her.

"He said that Wellbourne could not survive another scandal—that a word to the Duke of Rutland or any of the local masters of the hunt would ruin us." She finished her sherry in one last eye-stinging gulp, then set down the glass.

Sebastian took her hands, his skin warm and roughened against hers. "Jane, you are not yet of age. Promises made by a minor are not binding in the eyes of the law. His breach of promise suit has no foundation."

Jane digested this. "That scoundrel."

"Exactly. You had no way of knowing not to take his threat seriously. He was counting on your youth and inexperience, and he was counting on you being here alone." He frowned. "Where the devil is your mother, anyway?"

"I am not certain, but I suspect she has gone to Bath for the summer, My father left her a small set of rooms there in addition to the dower cottage here at Wellbourne. After what happened in London, I suppose she had no desire to face her friends here."

"And rumor has it that I am still in Town, having abandoned you," Sebastian said with a growl. He muttered something else under his breath, too softly for her to hear.

"He said you would not help me. I almost believed him," she admitted.

The viscount reached up and brushed a stray lock of hair away from her eyes. "I am glad you trusted me enough to confide in me."

The tender gesture made Jane's heart lurch sideways. "I had to start somewhere."

He kissed her gently, tenderly, one arm slipping around her waist and drawing her closer to him until she could rest her head upon his chest. She sighed and leaned against him, taking comfort in the strong, steady beat of his heart. There, nestled in the circle of his arms, the triangle of bare skin at his throat warm against her cheek, she felt secure. She felt—loved. If only that were true. A tear slipped from beneath her lashes.

Sebastian pressed another kiss to the crown of her

head and eased his arms away. "I want you to stay here until I get back," he said roughly.

She lifted her head. "Where are you going?"

Her tears distracted him; he brushed them away with his thumb. "What's all this?"

"Nothing," she replied hastily, attempting to blot them with her cuff.

He smiled. "And neither of us with a handkerchief—again. Will we never learn?"

She would not be put off. "Where are you going, Sebastian?"

"A bath first, I think, and then a change of clothes. After all, I cannot very well pay a call on Mr. Wingate looking like a stable boy."

"I am going with you," she declared.

He smiled again, but this time there was no mirth in it. "Not this time, my dear. There are no doubt going to be some very coarse, very ugly words exchanged, and I want you to have no part of it."

The steel in his voice made her shiver. "What do you intend to do?"

"Do not fret—I am not by nature a violent man. I merely intend to make Mr. Wingate see the folly of his actions."

"And if he does not?"

"Well, then, I shall have to challenge him to a duel."

He said it seriously—no teasing, no devil-may-care raillery.

Jane's vision began to blur at the edges. "Sebastian—no! He may not look it, but he is a crack shot. I have seen him shoot. He will kill you!"

The viscount bent down and kissed her again.

"I doubt it will come to that. Now, go find yourself a handkerchief, and let me deal with Mr. Wingate."

*   *   *

The reedy, gray-haired butler showed Sebastian down
a long hall and into Augustus Wingate's study, then vanished with a speed the viscount would not have expected
of the elderly servant. Obviously, he did not wish to be
present for what was about to happen.

Sebastian cast a jaundiced eye about the room. No
doubt Wingate had intended this room to reflect his sporting prowess; several sets of antlers were mounted on the
wall, and a moth-eaten bearskin rug sprawled over the
floor. Several skulls, lumps of bleached bone that might
have once been foxes or badgers, adorned the shelves of
a bookcase by the window. A side chair, the seat covered
with what must be a ragged deer hide, crouched in one
corner. The windows appeared as though they had not
been cleaned in years, and the whole room smelled very
strongly of dog. The viscount was appalled.

The overfed hunter himself lounged in a similarly
overfilled leather chair by the fire, an old pointer at his
feet. The dog raised its graying muzzle and thumped its
tail on the carpet a few times as Sebastian entered.

The two men eyed each other.

This was Augustus Wingate? Sebastian could never
imagine his tiny wife married to such a mountain of a
man. Egad, she would run the risk of being crushed into
a damp spot on the sofa if she sat too near him. What in
the bloody blue blazes had she been thinking?

Wingate huffed a great sigh and heaved his bulky body
from the chair. "Good afternoon, Langley," he intoned. "I
confess I am surprised to see you."

The viscount spared the man a brief nod. "Yes, I am
certain you are."

Wingate slanted him a sly look. "Thought you were

still in London. How long have you been in Leicester-shire?"

"Long enough," Sebastian replied tightly. "I shall be brief, sir. I know about your visit to my wife, and I am here to state unequivocally that you will receive not so much as a farthing from her."

"Oho," wheezed Wingate with amusement, sitting down again. His chair creaked a protest. "Told you about that, did she? 'Pon rep, the chit's got bottom."

"So you do not deny threatening her?"

Anyone of Sebastian's acquaintance would have recognized that dangerous tone and known to be on their guard. This oaf, however, appeared to possess no such discernment.

"On the contrary, Langley. I did not threaten anyone. I merely pointed out to the girl that she had violated our contract and that I am owed fair compensation as a result. A business arrangement, that's all."

"If you call blackmail a business arrangement, sirrah, then I should not hesitate to call the law on you," the viscount replied in glacial tones.

Malice glittered in Wingate's nearly colorless eyes. "Go ahead. The magistrate's m' brother-in-law. Don't think he would take too kindly to some misguided London buck coming up here and interfering with his duties."

"Indeed?" Sebastian nudged the head of the bear rug with the toe of his boot; the creature's fangs gleamed a dull yellow in the firelight. "Then that is why Jane took your threat to heart, even though legally you haven't a leg to stand on. I did point that out to her."

Wingate chuckled. "Ah, well. Can't blame a fellow for trying to get what's his."

"Actually—yes, I can."

Wingate squinted up at him. "I say, Langley why don't

we discuss this business man to man. The girl *did* agree to marry me, then reneged. That must count for something."

Sebastian forced back another surge of anger. Let the lout hoist himself on his own petard. "What did you have in mind?"

"You won't be needing her land. Your father's got estates to spare. A provincial stud farm like Wellbourne cannot possibly hold any interest for a gentleman like you."

"Why does everyone assume it would not?" the viscount murmured.

"Well, it doesn't, does it?"

"As it happens—yes, it does. Jane is very attached to Wellbourne, and I would not dream of making her part with it. Oh . . . and if you try to intimidate her again, you will have to go through me first. I have every intention of staying in Leicestershire to help my wife manage Wellbourne Grange."

Wingate's eyes narrowed until they became mere glints of light in the folds of his face. "You're a gambler, Langley. I have heard all the gossip about you from London. You're always punting on the River Tick. In need of the ready, are you? Good—then I'll give you a fair price for Wellbourne. All of it. Lands, buildings, and horse-flesh."

"Do you think that the way you've treated my dear wife gives me any incentive to sell?" Sebastian asked, one eyebrow arched.

A dull flush stained Wingate's cheeks. "Don't tell me you're *fond* of the chit!" he blustered.

"Quite fond. And very protective when her oafish bully of a neighbor tries to blackmail her."

Wingate squinted at him, and a crafty look slid over

his features. "I say, Langley—I'm rather surprised at you."

"In what way?"

"Defending damaged goods with such forcefulness. But she has a way of getting under one's skin, does she not? Jane may not be much to look at, but she's a passionate little thing. Full of enthusiasm for—physical activity."

"Careful what you say, sir," Sebastian warned with a growl. "I will not hear any slander against my wife."

Wingate chortled. "It's not slander if it's true. I'm sure you've seen for yourself what a skilled—rider—she is."

The image of Jane writhing naked atop this great mound of flesh made his blood turn to molten iron in his veins. God in heaven, but his fingers itched to draw this bounder's cork! Then he paused, thought about it again—and began to laugh.

"What's so funny?" demanded Wingate.

"You must be an even greater idiot than I suspected," the viscount drawled, still chuckling. "Anyone who truly knew Jane would realize she would never allow a tub of guts like you to touch her, in or out of wedlock." He glanced at Wingate's paunch and shuddered. "Egad, what a ghastly thought."

Blowing hard like a bull in heat, Wingate hauled himself to his feet. The old dog whined and scuttled into the corner.

"How dare you," Wingate fumed. "I'll not let you insult me in me own house!"

"Strange, but you showed no such hesitation with my wife."

"I demand satisfaction, sir."

Sebastian allowed himself a thin smile. "Then you shall have it."

"Name your weapon."

"Pistols."

A slow, calculated smile oozed across Wingate's face. "So be it. I trust that dawn tomorrow is convenient?"

"It is."

"Good. I will have my second call upon yours to arrange the details."

"Agreed. And now, if our business is concluded, sir, I will take my leave." He spared his host a brief nod.

"I'm going to kill you, Langley," Wingate declared. "I'm going to enjoy having Wellbourne Grange *and* your wife."

Though he longed to put his hands around the man's neck and throttle him, Sebastian refused to give Wingate the satisfaction of his anger. Besides—his hands would never fit around the fellow's neck.

Instead, he merely lifted an eyebrow and swept the man from head to toe with a contemptuous gaze.

"You are not man enough for either, sir, though not for lack of trying."

The viscount could still hear Wingate bellowing when he strode through the front door and suddenly felt an immense swell of pity for the man's dog.

The heady thrill he had received from the confrontation with Augustus Wingate began to wane as his carriage trundled back toward Wellbourne. Where was he going to get a second for this damned duel? If Nigel were here— or even Jace, come to think of it—he would ask either of them without hesitation. Perhaps Finley, the steward, would do him the honor; he had earned the man's respect, however grudging, over the past weeks.

His wife presented a thornier problem.

He had not been entirely truthful with her when he had said he doubted this matter would end in a duel; when she told him what Wingate had done, grass for breakfast had become the only option. Of course he could not have come out and said it so baldly. He could not in good conscience add to her worries.

But if by chance she did discover his plans, she would wish to be there, and the last thing he wanted was for Jane to watch him get himself killed. Not that he had any intention of doing so, mind you, but Wingate had obviously had a great deal of practice shooting at small targets — and hitting them. It never served a man to underestimate his opponent. The possibility existed, however slight. He needed to keep her as far away as he could.

Question was — how in the devil was he supposed to do that?

Chapter Ten

When Sebastian returned to the house, Jane was waiting for him. With a cry, she launched herself into his arms.

"There you are," he said with a chuckle. "Did you miss me so much?"

She smiled up at him, luxuriating in the feel of his arms around her. "Desperately." Then she sobered and placed her hands on his chest. "What did he say?"

He shrugged. "Oh, nothing of consequence."

Dread added another loop to the knot in her stomach. He had not told her the truth. Perhaps it was something in his cavalier attitude that betrayed him, or the fact that only an idiot would believe that he had confronted Augustus Wingate and nothing had come of it.

"You are going to duel with him." She made it a statement, not a question. "Do not lie to me, Sebastian, I beg of you."

His sunny grin evaporated. "Yes."

"I thought you told me it wouldn't come to that," she said accusingly.

"I said I *doubted* it would. There is a difference."

"Oh!" She pulled away from him, piqued. "How can

you play at this? This is no game! I told you, Augustus
is a deadly shot."

"So am I," he maintained. "What, you think all I did
was gamble when I lived in London? That would hardly
make me a very accomplished rogue, would it? I rode
every day, practiced fencing at Angelo's, and shot the
occasional wafer at Manton's."

She hesitated. "Why?"

"Why, what?"

"Why did you have to challenge him?"

His brow puckered. "Actually, he beat me to it and
challenged me first. But how could I not accept? The
man insulted you in the worst possible way. I would not
stand for that."

"I am not . . ." She turned her head to the side. "I am
not worth your life."

"Yes, you are. Look at me." He tucked his hand beneath her chin and forced her to meet his gaze. "No
woman deserves to be bullied and terrorized and black-
mailed, especially not in her own home. Especially not
my wife."

She shuddered at the memory of her former fiancé's
threats, the sneer on his fleshy lips, his arrogant cer-
tainty that she would comply with his demands.

"I do not know what he told you to induce you to
marry him," Sebastian continued, "but you deserve the
same measure of happiness as your sister."

"He told me . . ." She shivered again. "He told me
that I must be practical. Papa wanted me to marry someone who would not sell off Wellbourne but stay and help
me manage it. Augustus agreed to do just that. And he
said—he said that with my marked lack of beauty, I
would be fortunate if any man ever looked twice at
me—they would all be staring at Penelope. If I did not

wish to end up a lonely old maid, marriage to him was the best option. He said he was wealthy and well connected and that he wanted me."

"He wanted your property," Sebastian corrected gently.

"I know that now. Deep down, I think I knew it then, too. But I had just spent the evening as a wallflower at the Ainsleys' ball, and I was so unhappy. I believed him. I thought no one else in the world would want me."

"Oh, Jane." He gathered her into his arms once more. "To think that no one but your sister appreciated you for *you*. That must have been a dreadfully lonely feeling."

"Yes. Oh, yes. Pen always seemed to understand. If not for her, I probably would have run mad long before now." Her gaze searched his face. "Tell me . . . after everything that has happened, do you regret coming here?"

He gave her an insouciant grin. "Not for an instant. Well, I suppose there *were* a few brief moments, mostly when that dratted pitchfork was chafing blisters on my palms. But other than that, no."

She swallowed around the lump at the back of her throat, then asked the question she had feared to ask these past two weeks: "Do you miss London?"

"London, or the gambling?"

"Both, I suppose."

"Have I ever told you why I cultivated such a reputation as a gamester?" he asked.

She shook her head.

"I started at the tables to make my father angry. He did not approve of gambling; it was something my brother Alex never did—or did rarely, I should say—so of course I had to try it. The more I gambled—and the higher the stakes, the better—the angrier my father became. I saw that as a victory of a sort."

"And now?"

He paused. "Jace and Nigel and I grew up together. Three rogues. If one of us gambled, the other two followed suit, so to speak. Without them, the green baize holds little attraction. I gambled for the companionship, I suppose. Not the money or the thrill. Although I must admit that winning is infinitely preferable to losing."

Ever the incorrigible charm. Jane tried to smile, failed, then reached up to smooth her hand along his tanned, faintly stubbled cheek. "I could not bear to see anything happen to you."

"If it does, I am certain you will be able to find another stable boy," he quipped.

"Do not tease me!" she cried. "In spite of everything that went on in London, in spite of the dreadful things we said to each other, in spite of . . ." She thought of her List; she could do no less than follow her own advice. Now was her time for her to throw it away and follow her heart. "I have denied it to myself for so long, but I can do so no longer when I face losing you like this. I love you, Sebastian."

He opened his mouth to speak; she covered it with her hand, silencing him.

"I love you, and I do not need you to love me in return. This is enough."

He gently took her wrist and drew her hand away from his mouth. "I have no intention of dying tomorrow," he said quietly. "I asked you to give me a chance to make amends, and I'll be damned before I let a pudding-bag like Augustus Wingate deprive me of that opportunity."

"Sebastian . . ."

"Dearest Jane," he murmured, then kissed the palm of her hand. His lips trailed down to her wrist, to the sensitive spot where her pulse beat shallowly beneath the skin, and there traced small, maddening circles on her flesh with his tongue.

Jane gasped. Heat blazed through her veins from that point of contact. Her entire body turned molten; she was a living, liquid flame.

"Sebastian," she whispered.

He drew a ragged breath, then lifted his head. His eyes were the color of indigo. "You are my wife in name only," he murmured. "If anything should happen to me, you may not be protected from those who would try to take Wellbourne from you."

She wanted nothing more than to drown in those blue depths. "Then perhaps we should remedy the situation."

"Are you certain?"

"Yes." She touched his cheek. "But if you wish to make me your wife in every sense of the word, do it because you want to, not from any concern for my future."

"Do you know what you are asking?"

She smiled faintly. "I believe I am asking you to make love to me, husband."

With a groan, he claimed her mouth with his. No, not just claimed. Possessed, invaded, ravaged. His insistent tongue parted her lips and tasted her, devoured her. Sebastian's hunger drew the very breath from her, as though he was trying to pull her very essence into him.

At last he pulled his head away, his face flushed, then swung her into his arms.

"Sebastian," Jane murmured against his chest.

"Yes, love?"

"When is the duel to take place?"

"It no longer matters," he replied, then carried her up the stairs.

Sebastian woke some time in the middle of the night. He craned his neck toward the window, his heart leaping into his throat—no light shone through the crack in the curtains. He breathed a sigh of relief and relaxed back into the pillows. Good. Dawn was another few hours away.

The figure next to him in bed stirred, then burrowed closer to him. He smiled and brushed his wife's fine, silky hair away from her face. The passion promised by her kisses had been nothing compared to what he unleashed in her. Untouched she may have been, but her eagerness and curiosity more than made up for any lack of experience. She had seemed almost—desperate in her need for him.

Then again, he might be dead in a few hours, so he could understand the immediacy of her ardor. But her passion stemmed from only one source.

She loved him.

He had guessed it back in London, had thrown it in her face at the time—he could not think about that night without a hot flush of shame. This afternoon she had told him without hesitation, without requiring a similar declaration from him in return. She had given herself freely, expecting nothing from him.

Why had he not been able to divulge his own feelings?

He ran a finger over the petal-soft skin of her exposed shoulder, down the length of her upper arm, and back again. Strange how one's potentially imminent death triggered such bouts of introspection. Perhaps he wanted to spare her any greater pain in case he did fall to Augustus Wingate. Perhaps . . . perhaps he had not been honest with himself

He loved her.

The admission surprised him—he had never imagined anything like this would happen. He had played the part of the carefree rogue for so long that he considered his heart immune. And yet . . . here he was, lying next to his wife, unable to do anything but gaze at her with wondering eyes.

Who would have thought that he would fall for the intriguing imp who had crashed so unceremoniously into his garden? Not he, at first. And not Nigel, certainly. His friend would make it into a good joke and laugh at Sebastian's expense. The viscount slid a hand over his chin, the stubble rough and prickly against his palm. His father might have suspected when he paid that fateful call. The wily old stoat might have seen the signs in Sebastian even then. And Jace—Jace would understand. He could no longer be angry at his friend; he only wished he could tell him in person and mend any perceived rift that still lingered between them.

He reached down and traced the outline of Jane's delicate ear with his fingertip. No elf, this—just flesh and blood. His . . . for the rest of his life.

How long that would be, only God knew. He pulled her naked form closer to his and arranged the bedclothes over them both. He did not want to go back to sleep; he might wake up and discover this had all been a dream, and he could not bear that.

So he lay awake, listening to the silent night, Jane cradled close.

When at last the sky lightened from black to indigo to gray, the viscount slid out of bed. He dressed as quietly as he could, then took a sheet of paper from the writing table and scribbled a hurried note. He stared at the sleeping form in his bed, his heart in his throat.

"I love you, imp," he whispered, brushing his lips over her forehead. "Forgive me."

She moaned a little in her sleep but did not wake.

With one last, longing look, Sebastian opened the door and slipped from the room.

Perhaps the sensation of being in a strange bed was what roused her. Jane's eyelids rose slowly, languorously, as if weighted down with lead. She stretched, then groaned a little; her body ached in unfamiliar places, particularly in between—

She gasped and sat up. Her gaze flew to the space next to her; the indent of Sebastian's head remained in the pillow, but her husband was gone. Pale yellow light filtered through the opening in the curtains, and suddenly Jane could not breathe.

Dawn. Sebastian's absence.

The duel.

"Damn you!" she cried, vaulting out of bed. Had he done this on purpose? Had he made love to her so she would still be sleeping and thus out of the way and blissfully ignorant? How dare he! Did he really think he could keep her away?

A scrap of parchment on the bedside table caught her eye. She reached for it, the paper crackling beneath her fingers.

My dearest Jane,
   By the time you read this, I hope to have already returned to deliver the good news in person. If I have not, then I am dead, to the chagrin of us both. In that case, you must contact my solicitors in

London, Barton and Trent, immediately. I have sent them a revised copy of my will, and you shall be well looked after. Wellbourne shall be yours forever, along with all my worldly goods and possessions. Next, I would like you to pay a visit to my father, the Earl of Stanhope, who resides at Stanhope Abbey in Kent, and notify him of my demise. He is an unrepentant curmudgeon, but I have the feeling that the two of you will get along famously.

Do not mourn overmuch, I beg you. I should hate to see you waste the rest of your life pining over a rogue like me. Know that I loved you, and that in the end I tried to do what was best.

Your own,
Sebastian

The note fell from Jane's shaking fingers.
Know that I loved you.

Tears flooded her eyes and spilled over onto her cheeks. He could not have told her last night? He had to share this with her in a *note*, of all things?

He loved her.

She could not let him die!

There was still time to stop this madness. She started toward the door, determined and angry.

And naked.

With a startled yelp, she yanked a sheet from the bed, then twined it around herself. Clutching the material to her chest, she hurried down the hall to her own room, where she all but threw herself into her riding habit.

Her fingers trembled as she did up the buttons; she swore an unladylike oath at her own clumsiness. Her boots likewise conspired against her by refusing to go on her feet. She took a deep, steadying breath, then concentrated on putting them on properly. Then she grabbed her gloves and, her unbound hair streaming behind her, ran all the way down to the stables.

"Will!" she shouted. "Will, where are you?"

The head groom emerged from the stables and stared at her, openmouthed. Small wonder—she must look like a maenad, all wild hair and wild eyes. "Miss Jane? Is anything wrong?"

She whirled on him. "Where is my husband?"

Will took a step back. "He rode out of here about half an hour ago on Oriole, ma'am, with Mr. Finley and Mr. Monk in the dogcart. Thought it was a mite strange, but—"

"Finley? He is in on this? Did they say where they were going?"

"Something about the stream in the far pasture, but—hey, wait! Miss Jane! What in blazes is going on?"

Jane had already hurtled past him and into the stable, stopping only to grab Tamerlane's gear from the tack room. The big gray shied when she threw open the door to his stall, but she grabbed his halter and cross-tied him between opposite sides of the stall so he would stand still.

"No time for explanations, old fellow," she muttered, throwing first the saddle pad, then her sidesaddle, unceremoniously over his broad back. Her shaking fingers fumbled with the buckles on the girth until she was ready to scream with frustration.

"Let me help you, Miss Jane." Suddenly Will was there—loyal, steadfast Will who had put her on the back of her first pony—his gnarled hands sure and steady.

"Thank you," Jane said, unable to keep the quaver from her voice.

The saddle secure, Will slipped the bridle over Tamerlane's head and buckled it into place. Then he led the gelding out of the stable and cupped his hands, waiting.

Jane set one foot in his hands and let him boost her into the saddle.

"Please, Miss Jane, tell me what is happening," he pleaded.

"Augustus Wingate is going to kill my husband," she replied through her tears. She kicked her heel against Tamerlane's flank and took off at a gallop.

"Well, gentlemen, it seems we are all here," said Mr. Monk. "Are you certain there can be no reconciliation between you?"

"Not unless this greedy, tallow-faced bastard gets down on his knees and apologizes to my wife for all his insults, bullying, and blackmail," Sebastian replied in a pleasant, conversational tone.

Augustus Wingate flushed. "Go to hell, Langley."

Sebastian inclined his head in a mocking bow. "After you."

The seconds inspected the pistols; when they were assured everything was in order, they presented them to the duelists. Sebastian hefted the weapon in his hand. Rays from the rising sun glinted off the blued steel barrel. Soon this would all be over, and, if the Almighty had heard his prayers, he would still be alive.

He thought of Jane, sound asleep in his bed, and grinned. If everything went as he hoped, he could return to join her before she ever woke up. If not . . . His grin disappeared. If not, then he would go to his grave with one of the sweetest memories of his life. And Jane would still be safe.

He glanced over at Augustus Wingate, who appeared to be deep in conversation with his second, Sir Roger Ainsley. Sebastian then turned to his own man. His opponent had sneered at Sebastian's choice, but Mr. Finley had done him a great honor by coming here.

"There is still time to settle this, my lord," the steward said, his thin face pale and grim.

"You know as well as I that will never happen, sir," the viscount replied, and pulled the pistol's hammer back to half cock.

Mr. Finley ran a hand through his shock of grizzled hair. "What shall I tell her?"

Sebastian smiled. "Don't worry, Finley—I have already said everything she needs to hear."

"Are you ready, gentlemen?" asked Sir Roger.

"I am," grunted Wingate. "Let's get on with it."

"Indeed," Sebastian acknowledged, coming to stand back to back with his opponent.

"I shall count off ten paces," said Sir Roger, "at which point you shall turn and fire one shot each."

"That will be all I need," Wingate muttered. "Hope you said your good-byes to your wife, Langley."

"I'd advise you not be so hasty. You do, after all, present a very large target."

"Not if I shoot you first."

Sebastian did not reply, but shifted his hold on his pistol; his hands had grown clammy, and it was difficult to maintain a decent grip.

Sir Roger began the count, and he began to pace accordingly.

"One . . . two . . . three . . . four . . ."

I love you. Jane. I always will.

" . . . five . . . six . . . seven . . . eight . . . nine . . ."

"No!" someone shouted.

He started to turn around; the report of a pistol startled him. Something struck him hard in the back, knocking the breath from his lungs. Blazing agony followed—his body was on fire. His knees crumpled. The ground rushed toward his face.

Bloody hell.

Faster, faster!

Jane crouched low over Tamerlane's neck; her hair whipped about her face, getting into her eyes and mouth, mingling with strands of her gelding's black mane and the metallic taste of fear. Her heart beat a frantic cadence in time with the horse's hooves. They soared over hedgerows and fences, disturbing coveys of quail and grouse. The misty morning landscape rushed past in a blur of green; Jane could barely see any of it through the veil of her tears. All that mattered was that she get to the north pasture. Sweat beaded on her forehead.

"Fly, dear heart," she whispered to the horse.

Dear God, let her get there in time . . .

The field lay just over the next hill; she urged Tamerlane upward. As they were about to reach the top, the sound of a gunshot pierced her.

Oh—please, no . . . !

She crested the hill and reined the gelding to a halt. Below her in the field a small cluster of men stood grouped around a single prone figure.

Her pulse pounding in her ears, she strained to see who had fallen.

Then she realized that her husband lay crumpled on

the ground, a bloodstain blooming over his chest like a grotesque flower.

"Sebastian!" The scream tore from her throat like a living thing, and she sagged over the gelding's neck, weeping.

She had lost him.

Chapter Eleven

A woman's scream split the air like the cry of a hawk.

Sebastian opened his eyes. What the devil . . . ? He felt as though he'd been beaten all over with a cricket bat. He tried to sit up. Excruciating pain shot through his shoulder.

Finley restrained him. "Easy, now, my lord, none of that."

The viscount heard the tumultuous pounding of hooves. Over Finley's shoulder he saw Jane draw her rangy gelding to a sudden halt. She flung herself from the saddle, her hair flying about her head like a halo, her eyes huge gray pools of anguish, her bloodless lips parted.

"Sebastian?" she wavered.

"Good morning, dearest," he said woozily, giving her the best grin he could manage. God's teeth, his shoulder hurt. He saw what remained of her color drain away, and he added, "Finley, I think my wife is about to faint."

"No, I am not," she declared, kneeling by his side. She caressed his face, her hands cool against his skin. "Are you in pain? I thought—I thought . . ."

"The ball went straight through his shoulder," said Mr.

Talbot brusquely. He finished bandaging the wound. "A clean shot."

"Then he'll be all right?" Jane asked, her anxious face upturned.

The surgeon scowled, then nodded once. "He'll have the arm in a sling for a few weeks, but he should recover. Demmed foolish business, dueling."

"Thank God," she murmured, then leaned down and kissed him. If he hadn't felt so thumpingly awful, Sebastian would have pulled her down against him, but since he did, he had to settle for kissing her back.

"What—happened?" he inquired, when her lips finally left his.

His wife glared at the assembled men. "Yes—what happened?"

Mr. Finley glared at Sebastian's erstwhile opponent, who stood to one side, weak-kneed and shaking. "This fellow," he jerked his thumb at Wingate, "turned and fired early."

"I did not!" Augustus protested. Perspiration plastered his hair to his scalp. "You said ten, Sir Roger. I would swear to it!"

"You turned on nine," Sir Roger said quietly. "We all saw it, Augustus. There is no excuse."

"No—no! You said ten. I am certain you said ten," Wingate babbled. "You are my friend, Sir Roger. Please—"

"I just watched you try to murder a man," the baronet replied, stern and unsmiling. "I am not sure I know you any more."

"No—I would never—I just . . ." Wingate floundered like a drowning man.

Sebastian opened his mouth to utter a scathing retort, but his wife beat him to it.

"You turned early?" she demanded. She rose, noted that Sebastian's blood stained the sleeve of her riding habit, then focused her stormy gaze on her former betrothed.

Wingate held out a hand to her. "Jane—my darling, you must understand—I did this for *you!*"

Sebastian snorted. A fresh bolt of pain lanced through him, and he winced.

She bent down and retrieved something from the grass; the viscount recognized his discarded pistol. His discarded, still loaded pistol.

"Now, Miss Jane, don't do anything hasty," protested Mr. Finley.

She did not seem to hear him; her eyes drilled into Augustus Wingate.

"You would have murdered my husband, and you have the audacity to claim you did it for me?" she asked, a thread of ice running through her voice. She turned the pistol over in her hands, grasped the pommel, and slipped her finger through the trigger guard.

Wingate paled. "Please . . . Jane . . . !"

Her grim expression never wavered. "I should serve you the same way," she said.

"I'm sorry—I'm sorry—I did not mean—really— oh, God—do not—please!"

Sebastian reached out his good hand. "Jane . . ."

Jane glared a moment longer at Augustus Wingate, then uncocked the pistol's hammer and handed the weapon to her steward. "Mr. Finley, I trust you will take care of this. I must see my husband home."

Wingate fell to his knees, sobbing.

"Good for you," Sebastian murmured.

"What are we going to do with him?" Finley said,

crossing his arms over his chest and staring at Wingate with undisguised loathing.

"I would have to take him to the magistrate in the next county," Sir Roger mused, "since Mr. Wingate's brother-in-law serves in that capacity here. Even so, I am not certain the fellow could protect Augustus, even if he wanted to."

"I have a better idea," Sebastian said. Every eye swiveled in his direction. "Here . . . help me up."

Jane, the surgeon, and Mr. Finley maneuvered him to his feet. He stood there, swaying, propped against his wife for support.

The viscount met Sir Roger's gaze. "This man is a bully. He has terrorized the neighborhood with his gossip and his threats, but for all his bravado, he is nothing but a coward. I think a more fitting punishment would be to let the whole county know exactly what happened here this morning."

"What?" Wingate raised his head, his face pale with horror.

"Would serve him right," Finley grumbled. "Lots of folks would love to see him brought low."

Sir Roger gave a grudging nod.

"Word will be all over the county by tomorrow," Sebastian said to Wingate. "And then every insult, every threat, every malicious piece of gossip will come back to haunt you."

"What am I supposed to do then?" Augustus demanded petulantly, rising to his feet.

"I hear the continent is nice this time of year," Sebastian suggested with a lopsided grin. "You will not even have to worry about that Corsican upstart breathing down your neck." A wave of dizziness crashed over him, and he swayed heavily against Jane. "I think you had best get me home, my love."

Sir Roger bowed slightly. "I sincerely regret my part in this disastrous incident, my lord," he said. "Allow me to wish you a very speedy recovery."

"Thank you, Sir Roger," Sebastian murmured. "I am certain that you shall be seeing more of my wife and me in the future."

"I look forward to it."

Mr. Talbot turned Sebastian's cravat into a makeshift sling for his arm, which eased some of the throbbing pain. Then, with the assistance of Mr. Monk, Jane and Mr. Finley managed to get him to the dogcart. He lay with his head pillowed on Jane's lap. It felt like heaven.

As the dogcart started off his wife smoothed his hair back from his forehead, her eyes clouded.

"What is it, imp?" he croaked.

She bit at her lower lip. "Did you make love to me in order to keep me distracted from the duel?" she asked, her voice soft and anguished. "Please, Sebastian . . . I need to know."

He smiled, reaching up with his good hand to caress the softness of her cheek. "No. I made love to you because I wanted to before I died. Because I loved you."

Tears swelled in her beautiful eyes. "Oh, Sebastian . . ." She kissed him.

The dogcart jolted; he groaned against her lips.

"Are you all right?" she asked anxiously.

He grinned. "I'm fine as long as you kiss me. So keep it up, love. It's a long ride home."

Her apprehension melted. "You are incorrigible, sir," she murmured.

"And you prefer me that way. Kiss me."

She smiled and did as he asked.

*   *   *

The butler appeared in the doorway of Jane's bed-chamber, his face pale. "Ah—Miss Jane—forgive me for interrupting you and his lordship, but . . ."

"Hand me that pillow, Meg." Jane gently propped another bolster behind her husband's head, then turned toward the door. "Yes, what is it, Huxley?"

Before the manservant could reply, a shrill, strident voice echoed from the vestibule below.

"Will *someone* tell me what is going on here? I demand to know this instant. How dare you treat me like a stranger in my own home!"

Huxley cleared his throat and looked as though he wished himself far, far away. "Lady Portia has arrived, ma'am."

A shiver skittered its way up her spine. Jane and Meg exchanged significant glances; Meg winced.

"Wha—? What's all this?" Sebastian lifted his head and frowned. "That sounded suspiciously like your mother. Have we been invaded? Shall I call in the troops?"

Jane smoothed her fingers across his forehead. "Nothing to worry about, my love. Rest, and I shall deal with her."

He tried to sit up. "Deal with that harpy? Alone? Oh, no. I am going with you."

"You, sir, have a hole in your shoulder, and I refuse to let you out of this bed." She pressed him back into the pillows. "I will go and talk to my mother."

"Are you certain?" he asked, clearly troubled.

"The battle between us has been brewing for a long time, my love. And I need to fight it alone. If I do not do this now, I will never be able face myself in the mirror."

He nodded and relaxed, a slight smile on his mobile mouth. "I understand."

"Lady Portia wishes her bags brought to her room," the butler said in an apologetic manner. "Shall I have the footmen see to it?"

"No, Huxley." Jane rose and smoothed her skirts. "I must speak with my mother first."

She descended the stairs with slow, deliberate steps. Her mother stood in the center of the vestibule, surrounded by her multitude of baggage, as fashionably dressed as ever in her carriage ensemble of sea-green corded muslin with fine Mechlin lace at the collar and cuffs. The ostrich plumes on her bonnet bobbed as she stamped her foot in frustration.

"Good day, ma'am," Jane said in a studiously neutral tone.

Lady Portia looked up and scowled, her lips pinched. "Well, it's about time. Gracious, look at you! You look like something the dog has dragged through the mud."

"How lovely to see you, too, Mama," Jane replied quietly. She halted on the bottom step.

"And what is that on your sleeve? Goodness, do you know how much that habit cost me?"

Jane glanced down; Sebastian's blood stained the cuffs and one sleeve of her riding habit. She swallowed hard. "It's blood."

"Blood?" Lady Portia pulled off her kidskin gloves. "Heavens, Jane, I do not know what I am supposed to do with you. What now, some sort of accident in those ghastly stables?"

"No, ma'am," Jane retorted. "What brings you here?"

Her mother grew livid. "How dare you use that tone with me! Wretched, ill-mannered girl. You are fortunate anyone deigned to marry you at all, much less the man I had in mind for Penelope."

Ordinarily she would retreat into silence when faced with Lady Portia's anger, but what she had been through today gave her courage. She had withstood seeing her husband shot; she could withstand her mother's temper tantrums. "If you have come here simply to intimidate me, Mother, then you have wasted your time."

Lady Portia's eyes hardened to chips of blue ice. "I will thank you to keep a civil tongue in your head, my girl."

"You need not speak to me as if I am a green miss, Mother. I am married, after all. Now what do you want?"

"What do I—? Of all the effrontery. I have come home. Now, where are all the dratted servants? I want my bags taken up to my rooms directly."

Jane swallowed hard. She must not waver. She straightened. "This is no longer your home, ma'am."

"Well, of course it is," Lady Portia scoffed. "I belong here."

Jane clenched her fingers in her skirt to still their shaking. "Do you? Then where were you when we lost five pregnant mares to disease in one season and struggled to pay the staff? Where were you when Pharaoh threw Papa and trampled him? Where were you this past month, when my husband was in London and I was left alone to manage this estate by myself?"

Lady Portia's nostrils flared. "How dare you! I am your mother!"

Jane stood her ground. "Yes, and for that I owe you my gratitude. But the way you have treated Penelope and me over the years, along with the abominable disdain with which you treated my father, does not entitle you to my love or my respect. You are welcome to stay here until the rest of your things can be transported to the dower cottage. After that, Lady Portia, I no longer want you in this house."

"Why, you impudent little baggage, how dare you—"

"I must remind you, ma'am, that my father left Wellbourne Grange to me in his will, just as he left you the dower cottage and the rooms in Bath."

Tears began to well in her mother's eyes. "How can you be so unfeeling?"

"On the contrary—I have a great many feelings, and I will not let you take advantage of them. I will no longer allow you to badger me or bludgeon me with guilt to get what you want."

Lady Portia's tears vanished in a trice. "I will not permit you to treat me in this shameful manner. You are my daughter. You should be grateful I gave birth to you at all."

"You have already played that card, ma'am. I am through with your selfish bullying; it will not fadge." She hoped she sounded as brave as her words.

Her mother glared at her, the full force of her malice shining from her eyes. "This is *my* house, and I am still mistress here. I am your mother, and I will thank you to remember your place. Now go upstairs to your room. I shall deal with you later."

Jane quailed beneath the force of that stare; she could feel it eating away at her resolve. Her stomach roiled.

"*Your* house, ma'am? I beg to differ with you."

Jane whirled. Sebastian stood at the top of the stairs, his arm in a sling, his face pale, his eyes ablaze with blue fury.

Lady Portia gaped at him. "What are *you* doing here? I thought you were in London."

"I live here. This is my home. When I married your

daughter, her property became mine by law, a fact which you seem to have conveniently forgotten."

Jane climbed the stairs to stand beside him. Had he suspected that she could not stand up to her mother? Tears of shame stung her eyes; she blinked them away. "What are you doing here? You should be in bed."

Sebastian grazed her chin with the pad of his thumb and gave her the lazy, lopsided smile that first won her heart. "I merely came to show my dear wife how much I love her and that I will support her no matter what difficulties she may face."

Warmth flooded Jane's soul. "I love you," she whispered.

"I know. I will always be here for you, Jane. What strength I have is yours."

"What is all this?" Lady Portia demanded. "What are you whispering about?"

Jane turned and lifted her chin. "You must excuse my husband's appearance; he is recovering from a wound he received defending my honor."

"A duel?" Lady Portia gasped, one hand to her breast. "Oh, good gracious! Whatever will the neighbors think? Oh, the scandal! Well, all I can say is that it's a good thing I came when I did. With my connections, I can save us all from complete and total ruin."

Sebastian's silent presence at her back bolstered her flagging courage; Jane knew what she had to do. "No, Mother."

"What do you mean, 'no'?" Lady Portia demanded.

"I should not expect you to recognize the significance of that word, since you have not heard it often. It means you shall not be staying here. I will ask Michael and Thomas to take your things to your rooms, and then instruct Huxley to begin moving your belongings to the dower cottage."

"You wretched little hussy—"

"Before I do," Jane continued quietly, "tell me one thing—why do you despise me so?"

"I cannot fathom your meaning," Lady Portia replied with a sniff.

"'Tis a simple enough question. What have I ever done to offend you?"

Her mother's eyes narrowed. "How could you not offend me? How could a woman of my beauty and breeding not be offended by giving birth to such a—a plain and ungainly creature?"

Jane began to tremble. "You hate me because I am a blot on your pride?"

"I do not expect you to understand. Your father never did, either, but he was a fool. You take after him in that respect."

Understanding flared. "That's it, isn't it? You were jealous of the affection Papa felt for me, when you had deemed me unworthy." Jane stared at her mother, stunned. "You hated me for diverting his attention, and you hated him because you were no longer the sole focus of his love. You could forgive Penelope, because she was beautiful like you. But you could never forgive me."

"Believe what you will," huffed Lady Portia. "It hardly matters to me."

"But it matters to *me*. It matters very much. All my life you have belittled me, told me I was ugly and worthless. I am none of those things, and my husband's love has made me see that."

Jane felt Sebastian move closer to her; his warm, calloused hand enveloped hers.

"Well, this is outside of enough!" Lady Portia

snapped. "I refuse to remain under the same roof with a heartless, presumptuous girl who is no better than she should be. I wash my hands of you, something I should have done a long time ago." With that, she turned on her delicate slippered heel and marched out the front door to her carriage.

Jane sagged against the stair railing. She had lost her father three years ago; now she had just lost her mother. She straightened. No, that was not true—she had never really had a mother. She had a cold, selfish woman who never truly cared about anyone but herself.

Oh, Pen, you would be proud of me. I finally stood up for us both.

Sebastian smiled at her. "Well done, Jane."

She shuddered. "I cannot believe I just threw my own mother out of the house."

"You did not throw her. She walked of her own accord. For that I would salute the conquering heroine, but if I did I suspect she would have my guts for garters."

Jane smiled back, although she felt drained. "I am too weary for much of anything, I fear."

He slipped his good arm around her shoulders. "Come here."

She allowed him to pull her close, careful not to jar his wound.

"You did what you felt you had to do," he murmured against her hair.

"I wish . . ." Jane bit her lip. "I wish it had not come to this. She is my mother."

"Yes," Sebastian agreed, "but she was poisoning you. My father told me the reasons behind his treatment of me; I can appreciate his motives, if not the way he acted on them. We might be able to understand each other some day. But your mother . . . I do not think she will ever admit that what she did, the way she treated you and your sister and your father, was wrong."

She nodded. Although the thought made her unhappy, she knew Sebastian was right. Her mother would never admit any fault, even when confronted with the facts.

"Besides," he continued, "I don't think she would be able to get over the scandal of a viscount working in the stables. Though I fear I will not be able to hold a pitchfork any time soon."

"That's quite all right," Jane replied, and traced a finger over his lips. "You need never use a pitchfork again, if you so choose."

"What, you have other plans for me?" He winked at her.

"As a matter of fact," she murmured with a wicked grin of her own, "yes, I do. And I think you will approve of them."

Sebastian sobered, his blue gaze searching her face. "You will always have me, imp."

Jane smiled. "We will always have each other." And she kissed him.

Epilogue

"I just received a letter from Nigel," Sebastian announced.

Jane rolled her eyes and put another dab of marmalade on her scone. "What is he up to now? Blinding the populace of London with a new waistcoat? Making fun of the latest crop of wallflowers?"

The viscount grinned. "You do not think very highly of Nigel, do you?"

"He called me a mousy little antidote on more than one occasion. He is smug, arrogant, rude, and insufferably pompous. And those are his *good* points."

Sebastian's grin did not waver. "Are you not the least bit curious as to what he has to say?"

Jane set down her scone. "Oh, all right. You won't stop grinning at me until you do."

"But you like the way I grin at you."

"Read, or I shall loft this scone at your head."

"Well, I shall spare you the details—and all the invective involved. Egad, he *must* be upset."

"Will you stop teasing me?" Jane demanded. Her hand hovered over the scone.

Sebastian laughed. "All right, all right. Apparently, he paid so much attention to your mother while we were in London that Lady Portia now believes herself in love with him."

Jane nearly inhaled her tea; she gasped, then began to cough. "Oh. My."

"Worse yet," he continued, "she is convinced that he returns her affection. He has fled over half of England trying to avoid her, but she will not relent. She wants him to marry her."

"Marry her? Poor Nigel. I think I actually feel sorry for him. When Lady Portia decides she wants something, she will not be gainsaid."

"Ah, and here is something else. His grandmother, the Dowager Duchess of Wexcombe, wants to marry him off to the daughter of an earl whose estate marches with his."

"Oh . . . that sounds too familiar for comfort," Jane said, and made a face. "Does the thought of marriage itself horrify him, or is it that everyone seems to want to choose a bride for him?"

"Nigel is a confirmed bachelor. Wild horses could not drag him to the altar."

Jane rose from her chair and came to look over her husband's shoulder at the cramped, hastily written script on the letter.

"Marriage is not so bad when you find the right person," she commented, casting a sideways glance at Sebastian's handsome profile.

"Is that so?" The viscount swept her off her feet and into his lap.

"Behave yourself, sir!" Jane sputtered in mock outrage. "We have only just removed your bandage; I will not have you injuring yourself again."

"Have *you* found the right person, madam?"

She smiled up at him, bathed in the radiant glow of his deep, slate blue eyes. "I suppose I have. Would you like to hear the list of his merits?"

He grimaced. "As long as you do not mention his drawbacks. Otherwise we might be here all day."

"Of his merits, I find him . . . handsome. Charming — make that very charming. Honorable. Brave. Passionate. And virile."

"Virile?" Sebastian raised an eyebrow.

"Virile," she confirmed. "The product of which will arrive in about seven months."

"A babe?" A slow smile spread across his face. "Really?"

"For a man who prides himself on his wit, dearest, you can be remarkably dense."

"But you cannot fault my love for you," he murmured, pulling her close.

Jane smiled and kissed him. "No, my love. Never that. That is your greatest merit of all."

Allison Lane

"A FORMIDABLE TALENT...
MS. LANE NEVER FAILS TO
DELIVER THE GOODS."
—*ROMANTIC TIMES*

THE NOTORIOUS WIDOW
0-451-20166-3

When a scoundrel tires to tarnish a young widow's reputation, a valiant Earl tries to repair the damage—and mend her broken heart...

BIRDS OF A FEATHER
0-451-19825-5

When a plain, bespectacled young woman keeps meeting the handsome arbiter of fashion for London society, Lord Wylie, she feels she is not his equal. It will take a public scandal, and a private passion, to bring them together.